THE MASTER MIND OF MARS

Also by Edgar Rice Burroughs and available in the NEL series:

PIRATES OF VENUS
GODS OF MARS
SYNTHETIC MEN OF MARS
ESCAPE ON VENUS
A PRINCESS OF MARS
JOHN CARTER OF MARS
LOST ON VENUS
SWORDS OF MARS
CARSON OF VENUS
FIGHTING MAN OF MARS
LLANA OF GATHOL
WIZARD OF VENUS

The Master Mind of Mars

EDGAR RICE BURROUGHS

NEW ENGLISH LIBRARY
TIMES MIRROR

First published by Methuen & Co. Ltd. in 1939
Second impression 1952
First Four Square edition 1962
Reprinted 1964

*

FIRST NEL PAPERBACK EDITION SEPTEMBER 1972
Reprinted April 1973

*

NEL Books are published by New English Library Limited from Barnard's Inn, Holborn, London, EC1. Made and printed in Great Britain by Love & Malcomson Ltd., Redhill, Surrey.

45001163 1

A LETTER

HELIUM, June 8th, 1925.

MY DEAR MR. BURROUGHS,

It was in the Fall of nineteen-seventeen at an officers' training camp that I first became acquainted with John Carter, War Lord of Barsoom, through the pages of your novel *A Princess of Mars*. The story made a profound impression upon me and while my better judgement assured me that it was but a highly imaginative piece of fiction, a suggestion of the verity of it pervaded my inner consciousness to such an extent that I found myself dreaming of Mars and John Carter, of Dejah Thoris, of Tars Tarkas and of Woola as they had been entities of my own experience rather than the figments of your imagination.

It is true that in those days of strenuous preparation there was little time for dreaming, yet there were brief moments before sleep claimed me at night and there were my dreams. Such dreams! Always of Mars, and during my waking hours at night my eyes always sought out the Red Planet when he was above the horizon and clung there seeking a solution of the seemingly unfathomable riddle he has presented to the Earthman for ages.

Perhaps the thing became an obsession. I know it clung to me all during my training camp days and at night, on the deck of the transport, I would lie on my back gazing up into the red eye of the god of battle—my god—and wishing that, like John Carter, I might be drawn across the great void to the haven of my desire.

And then came the hideous days and nights in the trenches—the rats, the vermin, the mud—with an occasional glorious break in the monotony when we were ordered over the top. I loved it then and I loved the bursting shells, the mad, wild chaos of the thundering guns, but the rats and the vermin and the mud—God! how I hated them. It sounds like boasting, I know, and I am sorry; but I wanted to write you just the truth about myself. I think you will understand. And it may account for much that happened afterwards.

There came at last to me what had come to so many others upon those bloody fields. It came within the week that I had received my first promotion and my captaincy, of which I was greatly proud, though humbly so; realizing as I did my youth, the great responsibility that it placed upon me as well as the opportunities it offered, not only in service to my country but, in a personal way, to the men of my command. We had advanced a matter of two kilometres and with a small detachment I was holding a very advanced position when I received orders to fall back to the new line. That is the last that I remember until I regained consciousness after dark. A shell must have burst among us. What became of my men I never knew. It was cold and very dark when I awoke and at first, for an instant, I was quite comfortable—before I was fully conscious, I imagine—and then I commenced to feel pain. It grew until it seemed unbearable. It was in my legs. I reached down to feel of them, but my hand recoiled from what it found, and when I tried to move my legs I discovered that I was dead from the waist down. Then the moon came out from behind a cloud and I saw that I lay within a shell hole and that I was not alone—the dead were all about me.

It was a long time before I found the moral courage and the physical strength to draw myself up upon one elbow that I might view the havoc that had been done me. One look was enough, I sank back in an agony of mental and physical anguish—my legs had been blown away from midway between the hips and knees. For some reason I was not bleeding excessively, yet I know that I had lost a great deal of blood and that I was gradually losing enough to put me out of my misery in a short time if I were not soon found; and as I lay there on my back, tortured with pain, I prayed that they would not come in time, for I shrank more from the thought of going maimed through life than I shrank from the thought of death. Then my eyes suddenly focused upon the bright red eye of Mars and there surged through me a sudden wave of hope. I stretched out my arms towards Mars, I did not seem to question or to doubt for an instant as I prayed to the god of my vocation to reach forth and succour me. I knew that he would do it, my faith was complete, and yet so great was the mental effort that I made to throw off the hideous bonds of my mutilated flesh that I felt a momentary qualm of nausea and then a sharp click as of the snapping of a steel wire, and suddenly I stood naked upon two good legs looking down upon the bloody, distorted thing that had been I. Just for an instant did I stand thus before I turned my eyes aloft again to my star of destiny and with outstretched arms stood there in the cold of that French night—waiting.

Suddenly I felt myself drawn with the speed of thought through the trackless wastes of interplanetary space. There was an instant of extreme cold and utter darkness, then——

But the rest is in the manuscript that, with the aid of one greater than either of us, I have found the means to transmit to you with this letter. You and a few others of the chosen will believe in it—for the rest it matters not as yet. The time will come—but why tell you what you already know?

My salutations and my congratulations—the latter on your good fortune in having been chosen as the medium through which Earthmen shall become better acquainted with the manners and customs of Barsoom, against the time that they shall pass through space as easily as John Carter and visit the scenes that he has described to them through you, as have I.

Your sincere friend,
ULYSSES PAXTON,
Late Captain, —th Inf.,
U.S. Army.

THE HOUSE OF THE DEAD

I MUST have closed my eyes involuntarily during the transition for when I opened them I was lying flat on my back gazing up into a brilliant, sunlit sky, while standing a few feet from me and looking down upon me with the most mystified expression was as strange a looking individual as my eyes ever had rested upon. He appeared to be quite an old man, for he was wrinkled and withered beyond description. His limbs were emaciated; his ribs showed distinctly beneath his shrunken hide; his cranium was large and well developed, which, in conjunction with his wasted limbs and torso, lent him the appearance of top-heaviness, as though he had a head beyond all proportion to his body, which was, I am sure, really not the case.

As he stared down upon me through enormous, many-lensed spectacles I found the opportunity to examine him as minutely in return. He was, perhaps, five feet five in height, though doubtless he had been taller in youth, since he was somewhat bent; he was naked except for some rather plain and well-worn leather harness which supported his weapons and pocket pouches, and one great ornament, a collar, jewel studded, that he wore around his scraggy neck —such a collar as a dowager empress of pork or real estate might barter her soul for, if she had one. His skin was red, his scant locks grey. As he looked at me his puzzled expression increased in intensity, he grasped his chin between the thumb and fingers of his left hand and slowly raising his right hand he scratched his head most deliberately. Then he spoke to me, but in a language I did not understand.

At his first words I sat up and shook my head. Then I looked about me. I was seated upon a crimson sward within a high-walled enclosure, at least two, and possibly three, sides of which were formed by the outer walls of a structure that in some respects resembled more closely a feudal castle of Europe than any familiar form of architecture that comes to my mind. The façade presented to my view was ornately carved and of most irregular design, the roof line being so broken as to almost suggest a ruin, and yet the whole seemed harmonious and not without beauty. Within the enclosure grew a number of trees and shrubs, all weirdly strange and all, or almost all, profusely flowering. About them wound walks of coloured pebbles among which scintillated what appeared to be rare and beautiful gems, so lovely were the strange, unearthly rays that leaped and played in the sunshine.

The old man spoke again, peremptorily this time, as though repeating a command that had been ignored, but again I shook my head. Then he lay a hand upon one of his two swords, but as he drew the weapon I leaped to my feet, with such remarkable results that I cannot even now say which of us was the more surprised. I must have sailed ten feet into the air and back about twenty feet from where I had been sitting; then I was sure that I was upon Mars (not that I had for one instant doubted it), for the effects of the lesser gravity, the colour of the sward and the skin-hue of the red Martians I had seen described in the manuscripts of John Carter, those marvellous and as yet unappreciated contributions to the scientific literature of the world. There could be no doubt of it, I stood upon the soil of the Red Planet, I had come to the world of my dreams—to Barsoom.

So startled was the old man by my agility that he jumped a bit himself, though doubtless involuntarily, but, however, with certain results. His spectacles tumbled from his nose to the sward, and then it was that I discovered that the pitiful old wretch was practically blind when deprived of these artificial aids to vision, for he got to his knees and commenced to grope frantically for the lost glasses, as though his very life depended upon finding them in the instant Possibly he thought that I might take advantage of his helplessness and slay him. Though the spectacles were enormous and lay within a couple of feet of him he could not find them, his hands, seemingly afflicted by that strange perversity that sometimes confounds our simplest acts, passing all about the lost object of their search, yet never once coming in contact with it.

As I stood watching his futile efforts and considering the advisability of restoring to him the means that would enable him more readily to find my heart with his sword point, I became aware that another had entered the enclosure. Looking towards the building I saw a large red-man running rapidly towards the little old man of the spectacles. The newcomer was quite naked, he carried a club in one hand, and there was upon his face such an expression as unquestionably boded ill for the helpless husk of humanity grovelling, mole-like, for its lost spectacles.

My first impulse was to remain neutral in an affair that it seemed could not possibly concern me and of which I had no slightest knowledge upon which to base a predilection towards either of the parties involved; but a second glance at the face of the club-bearer aroused a question as to whether it might not concern me after all. There was that in the expression upon the man's face that betokened either an inherent savageness of disposition or a maniacal cast of mind which might turn his evidently murderous attentions upon me after he had dispatched his elderly victim, while, in outward appearance at least, the latter was a sane and relatively harmless individual. It is true that his move to draw his sword against me was not indicative of a friendly disposition towards me, but at least, if there were any choice, he seemed the lesser of two evils.

He was still groping for his spectacles and the naked man was almost upon him as I reached the decision to cast my lot upon the side of the old man. I was twenty feet away, naked and unarmed, but to cover the distance with my Earthly muscles required but an instant, and a naked sword lay by the old man's side where he had discarded it the better to search for his spectacles. So it was that I faced the attacker at the instant that he came within striking distance of his victim, and the blow which had been intended for another was aimed at me. I side-stepped it and then I learned that the greater agility of my Earthly muscles had its disadvantages as well as its advantages, for, indeed, I had to learn to walk at the very instant I had to learn to fight with a new weapon against a maniac armed with a bludgeon, or at least, so I assumed him to be and I think that it is not strange that I should have done so, what with his frightful show of rage and the terrible expression upon his face.

As I stumbled about endeavouring to accustom myself to new conditions, I found that instead of offering any serious opposition to my antagonist I was hard put to it to escape death at his hands, so often did I stumble and fall sprawling upon the scarlet sward; so that the duel from its inception became but a series of efforts, upon his part to reach and crush me with his great club, and upon mine to dodge and elude him. It was mortifying, but it is the truth. However, this did not last indefinitely, for soon I learned, and quickly too under the exigencies of the situation, to command my muscles, and then I stood my ground and when he aimed a blow at me, and I had dodged it, I touched him with my point and brought blood along with a savage roar of pain. He went more cautiously then, and taking advantage of the change I pressed him so that he fell back. The effect upon me was magical, giving me new confidence, so that I set upon him in good earnest, thrusting and cutting until I had him bleeding in a half-dozen places, yet taking good care to avoid his mighty swings, any one of which would have felled an ox.

In my attempts to elude him in the beginning of the duel we had crossed the enclosure and were now fighting at a considerable distance from the point of our first meeting. It now happened that I stood facing towards that point at the moment that the old man regained his spectacles which he quickly adjusted to his eyes. Immediately he looked about until he discovered us, whereupon he commenced to yell excitedly at us at the same time running in our direction and drawing his short-sword as he ran. The red-man was pressing me hard, but I had gained almost complete control of myself, and fearing that I was soon to have two antagonists instead of one I set upon him with redoubled intensity. He missed me by the fraction of an inch, the wind in the wake of his bludgeon fanning my scalp, but he left an opening into which I stepped, running my sword fairly through his heart. At least I thought that I had pierced his heart, but I had forgotten what I had once read in one of John Carter's manuscripts to the effect that all the Martian internal organs are not disposed identically with those of Earthmen. However, the immediate results were quite as satisfactory as though I had found his heart, for the wound was sufficiently grievous to place him *hors de combat*, and at that instant the old gentleman arrived. He found me ready, but I had mistaken his intentions. He made no unfriendly gestures with his weapon, but seemed to be trying to convince me that he had no intention of harming me. He was very excited and apparently tremendously annoyed that I could not understand him, and perplexed, too. He hopped about screaming strange sentences at me that bore the tones of peremptory commands, rabid invective and impotent rage. But the fact that he had returned his sword to its scabbard had greater significance than all his jabbering, and when he ceased to yell at me and commenced to talk in a sort of pantomime I realized that he was making overtures of peace if not of friendship, so I lowered my point and bowed. It was all that I could think of to assure him that I had no immediate intention of spitting him.

He seemed satisfied and at once turned his attention to the fallen man. He examined his pulse and listened to his heart, then, nodding his head, he arose and taking a whistle from one of his pocket pouches sounded a single loud blast. There emerged immediately from one of the surrounding buildings a score of naked red-men who came running towards us. None was armed. To these he issued a few curt orders, whereupon they gathered the fallen one in their arms and bore him off. Then the old man started towards the building, motioning me to accompany him. There seemed nothing else for me to do but obey. Wherever I might be upon Mars, the chances were a million to one that I would be among enemies; and so I was as well off here as elsewhere and must depend upon my own resourcefulness, skill and agility to make my way upon the Red Planet.

The old man led me into a small chamber from which opened numerous doors, through one of which they were just bearing my late antagonist. We followed into a large, brilliantly lighted chamber, wherein there burst upon my astounded vision the most gruesome scene that I ever had beheld. Rows up rows of tables arranged in parallel lines filled the room and with few exceptions each table bore a similar grisly burden, a partially dismembered or otherwise mutilated human corpse. Above each table was a shelf bearing containers of various sizes and shapes, while from the bottom of the shelf depended numerous surgical instruments, suggesting that my entrance upon Barsoom was to be through a gigantic medical college.

At a word from the old man, those who bore the Barsoomian I had wounded laid him upon an empty table and left the apartment. Whereupon my host, if so I may call him, for certainly he was not as yet my captor, motioned me forward. While he conversed in ordinary tones, he made two incisions in the body of my late antagonist; one, I imagine, in a large vein and one in an artery, to which he deftly attached the ends of two tubes, one of which was connected with an empty glass receptacle and the other with a similar receptacle filled with a colourless, transparent liquid resembling clear water. The connections made, the old gentleman pressed a button controlling a small motor, whereupon the victim's blood was pumped into the empty jar while the contents of the other was forced into the emptying veins and arteries.

The tones and gestures of the old man as he addressed me during this operation convinced me that he was explaining in detail the method and purpose of what was transpiring, but as I understood no word of all he said I was as much in the dark when he had completed his discourse as I was before he started it, though what I had seen made it appear reasonable to believe that I was witnessing an ordinary Barsoomian embalming. Having removed the tubes the old man closed the openings he had made by covering them with bits of what appeared to be heavy adhesive tape and then motioned me to follow him. We went from room to room, in each of which were the same gruesome exhibits. At many of the bodies the old man paused to make a brief examination or to refer to what appeared to be a record of the case, that hung upon a hook at the head of each of the tables.

From the last of the chambers we visited upon the first floor my host led me up an inclined runway to the second floor where there were rooms similar to those below, but here the tables bore whole rather than mutilated bodies, all of which were patched in various places with adhesive tape. As we were passing among the bodies in one of these rooms a Barsoomian girl, whom I took to be a servant or slave, entered and addressed the old man, whereupon he signed me to follow him and together we descended another runway to the first floor of another building.

Here, in a large, gorgeously decorated and sumptuously furnished apartment an elderly red-woman awaited us. She appeared to be quite old and her face was terribly disfigured as by some injury. Her trappings were magnificent and she was attended by a score of women and armed warriors, suggesting that she was a person of some consequence, but the little old man treated her quite brusquely, as I could see, quite to the horror of her attendants.

Their conversation was lengthy and at the conclusion of it, at the direction of the woman, one of her male escort advanced and opening a pocket pouch at his side withdrew a handful of what appeared to me to be Martian coins. A quantity of these he counted out and handed to the little old man, who then beckoned the woman to follow him, a gesture which included me. Several of her women and guard started to accompany us, but these the old man waved back peremptorily; whereupon there ensued a heated discussion between the woman and one of her warriors on one side and the old man on the other, which terminated in his proffering the return of the woman's money with a disgusted air. This seemed to settle the argument, for she refused the coins, spoke briefly to her people and accompanied the old man and myself alone.

He led the way to the second floor and to a chamber which I had not previously visited. It closely resembled the others except that all the bodies therein were of young women, many of them of great beauty. Following closely at the heels of the old man the woman inspected the gruesome exhibits with painstaking care. Thrice she passed slowly among the tables examining their ghastly burdens. Each time she paused longest before a certain one which bore the figure of the most beautiful creature I had ever looked upon; then she returned the fourth time to it and stood looking long and earnestly into the dead face. For a while she stood there talking with the old man, apparently asking innumerable questions, to which he returned quick, brusque replies, then she indicated the body with a gesture and nodded assent to the withered keeper of this ghastly exhibit.

Immediately the old fellow sounded a blast upon his whistle, summoning a number of servants to whom he issued brief instructions, after which he led us to another chamber, a smaller one in which were several empty tables similar to those upon which the corpses lay in adjoining rooms. Two female slaves or attendants were in this room and at a word from their master they removed the trappings from the old woman, unloosed her hair and helped her to one of the tables. Here she was thoroughly sprayed with what I presume was an antiseptic solution of some nature, carefully dried and removed to another table, at a distance of about twenty inches from which stood a second parallel table.

Now the door of the chamber swung open and two attendants appeared bearing the body of the beautiful girl we had seen in the adjoining room. This they deposited upon the table the old woman had just quitted and as she had been sprayed so was the corpse, after which it was transferred to the table beside that on which she lay. The little old man now made two incisions in the body of the old woman, just as he had in the body of the red-man who had fallen to my sword; her blood was drawn from her veins and the clear liquid pumped into them, life left her and she lay upon the polished ersite slab that formed the table-top, as much a corpse as the poor, beautiful, dead creature at her side.

The little old man, who had removed the harness down to his waist and been thoroughly sprayed, now selected a sharp knife from among the instruments above the tab e and removed the old woman's scalp, following the hair line entirely around her head. In a similar manner he then removed the scalp from the corpse of the young woman, after which, by means of a tiny circular saw attached to the end of a flexible, revolving shaft he sawed through the skull of each, following the line exposed by the removal of the scalps. This and the balance of the marvellous operation was so skilfully performed as to baffle description. Suffice it to say that at the end of four hours he had transferred the brain of each woman to the brain pan of the other. deftly connected the severed nerves and ganglia, replaced the skulls and scalps and bound both heads securely with his peculiar adhesive tape, which was not only antiseptic and healing but anaesthetic, locally, as well.

He now reheated the blood that he had withdrawn from the body of the old woman, adding a few drops of some clear chemical solution, withdrew the liquid from the veins of the beautiful corpse, replacing it with the blood of the old woman and simultaneously administering a hypodermic injection.

During the entire operation he had not spoken a word. Now he issued a few instructions in his curt manner to his assistants, motioned me to follow him, and left the room. He led me to a distant part of the building or series of buildings that composed the whole, ushered me into a luxurious apartment, opened the door to a Barsoomian bath and left me in the hands of trained servants. Refreshed and rested I left the bath after an hour of relaxation to find harness and trappings awaiting me in the adjoining chamber. Though plain, they were of good material, but there were no weapons with them.

Naturally I had been thinking much upon the strange things I had witnessed since my advent upon Mars, but what puzzled me most lay in the seemingly inexplicable act of the old woman in paying my host what was evidently a considerable sum to murder her and transfer to the inside of her skull the brain of a corpse. Was it the outcome of some horrible religious fanaticism, or was there an explanation that my Earthly mind could not grasp?

I had reached no decision in the matter when I was summoned to follow a slave to another and near-by apartment where I found my host awaiting me before a table loaded with delicious foods, to which, it is needless to say, I did ample justice after my long fast and longer weeks of rough army fare.

During the meal my host attempted to converse with me but, naturally, the effort was fruitless of results. He waxed quite excited at times and upon three distinct occasions laid his hand upon one of his swords when I failed to comprehend what he was saying to me, an action which resulted in a growing conviction upon my part that he was partially demented; but he evinced sufficient self-control in each instance to avert a catastrophe for one of us.

The meal over he sat for a long time in deep meditation, then a sudden resolution seemed to possess him. He turned suddenly upon me with a faint suggestion of a smile and dived headlong into what was to prove an intensive course of instruction in the Barsoomian language. It was long after dark before he permitted me to retire for the night, conducting me himself to a large apartment, the same in which I had found my new harness, where he pointed out a pile of rich sleeping silks and furs, bid me a Barsoomian goodnight and left me, locking the door after him upon the outside, and leaving me to guess whether I were more guest or prisoner.

PREFERMENT

THREE weeks passed rapidly. I had mastered enough of the Barsoomian tongue to enable me to converse with my host in a reasonably satisfactory manner, and I was also progressing slowly in the mastery of the written language of his nation, which is different, of course, from the written language of all other Barsoomian nations, though the spoken language of all is identical. In these three weeks I had learned much of the strange place in which I was half guest and half prisoner and of my remarkable host-jailer, Ras Thavas, the old surgeon of Toonol, whom I had accompanied almost constantly day after day until gradually there had unfolded before my astounded faculties an understanding of the purposes of the institution over which he ruled and in which he laboured practically alone; for the slaves and attendants that served him were but hewers of wood and carriers of water. It was his brain alone and his skill that directed the sometimes beneficent, the sometimes malevolent, but always marvellous activities of his life's work.

Ras Thavas himself was as remarkable as the things he accomplished. He was never intentionally cruel; he was not, I am sure, intentionally wicked. He was guilty of the most diabolical cruelties and the basest of crimes; yet in the next moment he might perform a deed that if duplicated upon Earth would have raised him to the highest pinnacle of man's esteem. Though I know that I am safe in saying that he was never prompted to a cruel or criminal act by base motives, neither was he ever urged to a humanitarian one by high motives. He had a purely scientific mind entirely devoid of the cloying influences of sentiment, of which he possessed none. His was a practical mind, as evidenced by the enormous fees he demanded for his professional services; yet I know that he would not operate for money alone and I have seen him devote days to the study of a scientific problem the solution of which could add nothing to his wealth, while the quarters that he furnished his waiting clients were overflowing with wealthy patrons waiting to pour money into his coffers.

His treatment of me was based entirely upon scientific requirements. I offered a problem. I was either, quite evidently, not a Barsoomian at all, or I was of a species of which he had no knowledge. It therefore best suited the purposes of science that I be preserved and studied. I knew much about my own planet. It pleased Ras Thavas' scientific mind to milk me of all I knew in the hope that he might derive some suggestion that would solve one of the Barsoomian scientific riddles that still baffle their savants; but he was compelled to admit that in this respect I was a total loss, not alone because I was densely ignorant upon practically all scientific subjects, but because the learned sciences on Earth have not advanced even to the swaddling-clothes stage as compared with the remarkable progress of corresponding activities on Mars. Yet he kept me by him, training me in many of the minor duties of his vast laboratory. I was entrusted with the formula of the 'embalming fluid' and taught how to withdraw a subject's blood and replace it with this marvellous preservative that arrests decay without altering in the minutest detail the nerve or tissue structure of the body. I learned also the secret of the few drops of solution which, added to the rewarmed blood before it is returned to the veins of the subject, revitalizes the latter and restores to normal and healthy activity each and every organ of the body.

He told me once why he had permitted me to learn these things that he had kept a secret from all others, and why he kept me with him at all times in preference to any of the numerous individuals of his own race that served him and me in lesser capacities both day and night.

'Vad Varo,' he said, using the Barsoomian name that he had given me because he insisted that my own name was meaningless and impractical, 'for many years I have needed an assistant, but heretofore I have never felt that I had discovered one who might work here for me wholeheartedly and disint restedly without ever having reason to go elsewhere or to divulge my secrets to others. You, in all Barsoom, are unique—you have no other friend or acquaintance than myself. Were you to leave me you would find yourself in a world of enemies, for all are suspicious of a stranger. You would not survive a dozen dawns and you would be cold and hungry and miserable—a wretched outcast in a hostile world. Here you have every luxury that the mind of man can devise or the hand of man produce, and you are occupied with work of such engrossing interest that your every hour must be fruitful of unparalleled satisfaction. There is no selfish reason, therefore, why you should leave me and there is every reason why you should remain. I expect no loyalty other than that which may be prompted by egoism. You make an ideal assistant, not only for the reasons I have just given you, but because you are intelligent and quick-witted, and now I have decided, after observing you carefully for a sufficient time, that you can serve me in yet another capacity—that of personal bodyguard.

'You may have noticed that I alone of all those connected with my laboratory am armed. This is unusual upon Barsoom, where people of all classes, and all ages and both sexes habitually go armed. But many of these people I could not trust armed as they would slay me; and were I to give arms to those whom I might trust, who knows but that the others would obtain possession of them and slay me, or even those whom I had trusted turn against me, for there is not one who might not wish to go forth from this place back among his own people—only you, Vad Varo, for there is no other place for you to go. So I have decided to give you weapons.

'You saved my life once. A similar opportunity might again present itself. I know that, being a reasoning and reasonable creature, you will not slay me, for you have nothing to gain and everything to lose by my death, which would leave you friendless and unprotected in a world of strangers where assassination is the order of society and natural death one of the rarest of phenomena. Here are your arms.' He stepped to a cabinet which he unlocked, displaying an assortment of weapons, and selected for me a long-sword, a short-sword, a pistol and a dagger.

'You seem sure of my loyalty, Ras Thavas,' I said.

He shrugged his shoulders. 'I am only sure that I know perfectly where your interests lie—sentimentalists have words: love, loyalty, friendship, enmity, jealousy, hate, a thousand others; a waste of words—one word defines them all: self-interest. All men of intelligence realize this. They analyse an individual and by his predilections and his needs they classify him as friend or foe, leaving to the weak-minded idots who like to be deceived the drooling drivel of sentiment.'

I smiled as I buckled my weapons to my harness, but I held my peace. Nothing could be gained by arguing with the man and, too, I felt quite sure that in any purely academic controversy I should get the worst of it; but many of the matters of which he had spoken had aroused my curiosity and one had reawakened in my mind a matter to which I had given considerable thought. While partially explained by some of his remarks I still wondered why the red-man from whom I had rescued him had seemed so venomously bent upon slaying him the day of my advent upon Barsoom, and so, as we sat chatting after our evening meal, I asked him.

'A sentimentalist,' he said. 'A sentimentalist of the most pronounced type. Why that fellow hated me with a venom absolutely unbelievable by any of the reactions of a trained, analytical mind such as mine; but having witnessed his reactions I became cognizant of a state of mind that I cannot of myself even imagine. Consider the facts. He was the victim of assassination—a young warrior in the prime of life, possessing a handsome face and a splendid physique. One of my agents paid his relatives a satisfactory sum for the corpse and brought it to me. It is thus that I obtain practically all of my material. I treated it in the manner with which you are familiar. For a year the body lay in the laboratory, there being no occasion during that time that I had use for it; but eventually a rich client came, a not overly prepossessing man of considerable years. He had fallen desperately in love with a young woman who was attended by many handsome suitors. My client had more money than any of them, more brains, more experience, but he lacked the one thing that each of the others had that always weighs heavily with the undeveloped, unreasoning, sentiment-ridden minds of young females—good looks.

'Now 378-J-493811-P had what my client lacked and could afford to purchase. Quickly we reached an agreement as to price and I transferred the brain of my rich client to the head of 378-J-493811-P and my client went away and for all I know won the hand of the beautiful moron; and 378-J-493811-P might have rested on indefinitely upon his ersite slab until I needed him or a part of him in my work, had I not, merely by chance, selected him for resurgence because of an existing need for another male slave.

'Mind you now, the man had been murdered. He was dead. I bought and paid for the corpse and all there was in it. He might have lain dead for ever upon one of my ersite slabs had I not breathed new life into his dead veins. Did he have the brains to view the transaction in a wise and dispassionate manner? He did not. His sentimental reactions caused him to reproach me because I had given him another body, though it seemed to me that, looking at the matter from a standpoint of sentiment, if one must, he should have considered me as a benefactor for having given him life again in a perfectly healthy, if somewhat used, body.

'He had spoken to me upon the subject several times, begging me to restore his body to him, a thing which, of course, as I explained to him, was utterly out of the question unless chance happened to bring to my laboratory the corpse of the client who had purchased his carcass—a contingency quite beyond the pale of possibility for one as wealthy as my client. The fellow even suggested that I permit him to go forth and assassinate my client, bringing the body back that I might reverse the operation and restore his body to his brain. When I refused to divulge the name of the present possessor of his body he grew sulky, but until the very hour of your arrival, when he attacked me, I did not suspect the depth of his hate complex.

'Sentiment is indeed a bar to all progress. We of Toonol are probably less subject to its vagaries than most other nations upon Barsoom, but yet most of my fellow countrymen are victims of it in varying degrees. It has its rewards and compensations, however. Without it we could preserve no stable form of government and the Phundahlians, or some other people, would overrun and conquer us; but enough of our lower classes have sentiment to a sufficient degree to give them loyalty to the Jeddak of Toonol and the upper classes are brainy enough to know that it is to their own best interests to keep him upon his throne.

'The Phundahlians, upon the other hand, are egregious

sentimentalists, filled with crass stupidities and superstitions slaves to every variety of brain-withering conceit. Why, the very fact that they keep the old termagant, Xaxa, on the throne brands them with their stupid idiocy. She is an ignorant, arrogant, selfish, stupid, cruel virago, yet the Phundahlians would fight and die for her because her father was Jeddak of Phundahl. She taxes them until they can scarce stagger beneath their burden, she misrules them, exploits them, betrays them, and they fall down and worship at her feet. Why? Because her father was Jeddak of Phundahl and his father before him and so on back into antiquity; because they are ruled by sentiment rather than reason; because their wicked rulers play upon this sentiment.

'She had nothing to recommend her to a sane person—not even beauty. You know, you saw her.'

'I saw her?' I demanded.

'You assisted me the day that we gave her old brain a new casket—the day you arrived from what you call your Earth.'

'She! That old woman was Jeddara of Phundahl?'

'That was Xaxa,' he assured me.

'Why, you did not accord her the treatment that one of the Earth would suppose would be accorded a ruler, and so I had no idea that she was more than a rich old woman.'

'I am Ras Thavas,' said the old man. 'Why should I incline the head to any other? In my world nothing counts but brain and in that respect, and without egotism, I may say that I acknowledge no superior.'

'Then you are not without sentiment,' I said, smiling. 'You acknowledge pride in your intellect!'

'It is not pride,' he said, patiently, for him, 'it is merely a fact that I state. A fact that I should have no difficulty in proving. In all probability I have the most highly developed and perfectly functioning mind among all the learned men of my acquaintance, and reason indicates that this fact also suggests that I possess the most highly developed and perfectly functioning mind upon Barsoom. From what I know of Earth and from what I have seen of you, I am convinced that there is no mind upon your planet that may even faintly approximate in power that which I have developed during a thousand years of active study and research. Rasoom (Mercury) or Cosoom (Venus) may possibly support intelligences equal to or even greater than mine. While we have made some study of their thought waves, our instruments are not yet sufficiently developed to more than suggest that they are of extreme refinement, power and flexibility.'

'And what of the girl whose body you gave to the Jeddara?' I asked, irrelevantly, for my mind could not efface the memory of that sweet body that must, indeed, have possessed an equally sweet and fine brain.

'Merely a subject! Merely a subject!' he replied with a wave of his hand.

'What will become of her?' I insisted.

'What difference does it make?' he demanded. 'I bought her with a batch of prisoners of war. I do not even recall from what country my agent obtained them, or from whence they originated. Such matters are of no import.'

'She was alive when you bought her?' I demanded.

'Yes. Why?'

'You—er—ah—killed her, then?'

'Killed her! No; I preserved her. That was some ten years ago. Why should I permit her to grow old and wrinkled? She would no longer have the same value then, would she? No, I preserved her. When Xaxa bought her she was just as fresh and young as the day she arrived. I kept her a long time. Many women looked at her and wanted her face and figure, but it took a Jeddara to afford her. She brought the highest price that I have ever been paid.

'Yes, I kept her a long time, but I knew that some day she would bring my price. She was indeed beautiful and so sentiment has its uses—were it not for sentiment there would be no fools to support this work that I am doing, thus permitting me to carry on investigations of far greater merit. You would be surprised, I know, were I to tell you that I feel that I am almost upon the point of being able to reproduce rational human beings through the action upon certain chemical combinations of a group of rays probably entirely undiscovered by your scientists, if I am to judge by the paucity of your knowledge concerning such things.'

'I would not be surprised,' I assured him. 'I would not be surprised by anything that you might accomplish.'

VALLA DIA

I LAY awake a long time that night thinking of 4296-E-2631-H, the beautiful girl whose perfect body had been stolen to furnish a gorgeous setting for the cruel brain of a tyrant. It seemed such a horrid crime that I could not rid my mind of it and I think that contemplation of it sowed the first seed of my hatred and loathing for Ras Thavas. I could not conjure a creature so utterly devoid of bowels of compassion as to even consider for a moment the frightful ravishing of that sweet and lovely body for even the holiest of purposes, much less one that could have been induced to do so for filthy pelf.

So much did I think upon the girl that night that her image was the first to impinge upon my returning consciousness at dawn, and after I had eaten, Ras Thavas not having appeared, I went directly to the storage room where the poor thing was. Here she lay, identified only by a small panel, bearing a number: 4296-E-2631-H. The body of an old woman with a disfigured face lay before me in the rigid immobility of death; yet that was not the figure that I saw, but instead, a vision of radiant loveliness whose imprisoned soul lay dormant beneath those greying locks.

The creature here with the face and form of Xaxa was not Xaxa at all, for all that made the other what she was had been transferred to this cold corpse. How frightful would be the awakening, should awakening ever come! I shuddered to think of the horror that must overwhelm the girl when first she realized the horrid crime that had been perpetrated upon her. Who was she? What story lay locked in that dead and silent brain? What loves must have been hers whose beauty was so great and upon whose fair face had lain the indelible imprint of graciousness! Would Ras

Thavas ever arouse her from this happy semblance of death?—far happier than any quickening ever could be for her. I shrank from the thought of her awakening and yet I longed to hear her speak, to know that that brain lived again, to learn her name, to listen to the story of this gentle life that had been so rudely snatched from its proper environment and so cruelly bandied by the hand of Fate. And suppose she were awakened! Suppose she were awakened and that I—— A hand was laid upon my shoulder and I turned to look into the face of Ras Thavas.

'You seem interested in this subject,' he said.

'I was wondering,' I replied, 'what the reaction of this girl's brain would be were she to awaken to the discovery that she had become an old, disfigured woman.'

He stroked his chin and eyed me narrowly. 'An interesting experiment,' he mused. 'I am gratified to discover that you are taking a scientific interest in the labours that I am carrying on. The psychological phases of my work I have, I must confess, rather neglected during the past hundred years or so, though I formerly gave them a great deal of attention. It would be interesting to observe and study several of these cases. This one, especially, might prove of value to you as an initial study, it being simple and regular. Later we will let you examine into a case where a man's brain has been transferred to a woman's skull, and a woman's brain to a man's. There are also the interesting cases where a portion of diseased or injured brain has been replaced by a portion of the brain from another subject; and, for experimental purposes alone, those human brains that have been transplanted to the craniums of beasts, and *vice versa,* offer tremendous opportunities for observation. I have in mind one case in which I transferred half the brain of an ape to the skull of a man, after having removed half of his brain, which I grafted upon the remaining part of the brain in the ape's skull. That was a matter of several years ago and I have often thought that I should like to recall these two subjects and note the results. I shall have to have a look at them—as I recall it they are in vault L-42-X beneath building 4-J-21. We shall have to have a look at them some day soon—it has been years since I have been below. There must be some very interesting specimens there that have escaped my mind. But come! Let us recall 4296-E-2631-H.'

'No!' I exclaimed, laying a hand upon his arm. 'It would be horrible.'

He turned a surprised look upon me and then a nasty, sneering smile curled his lips. 'Maudlin, sentimental fool!' he cried. 'Who dare say no to me?'

I laid a hand upon the hilt of my long-sword and looked him steadily in the eye. 'Ras Thavas,' I said, 'you are master in your own house; but while I am your guest treat me with courtesy.'

He returned my look for a moment but his eyes wavered. 'I was hasty,' he said. 'Let it pass.' That, I let answer for an apology—really it was more than I had expected—but the event was not unfortunate. I think he treated me with far greater respect thereafter; but now he turned immediately to the slab bearing the mortal remains of 4296-E-2631-H.

'Prepare the subject for revivication,' he said, 'and make what study you can of all its reactions.' With that he left the room.

I was now fairly adept at this work which I set about with some misgivings but with the assurance that I was doing right in obeying Ras Thavas while I remained a member of his entourage. The blood that had once flowed through the veins of the beautiful body that Ras Thavas had sold to Xaxa reposed in an hermetically sealed vessel upon the shelf above the corpse. As I had before done in other cases beneath the watchful eyes of the old surgeon I now did for the first time alone. The blood heated, the incisions made, the tubes attached and the few drops of life-giving solution added to the blood, I was now ready to restore life to that delicate brain that had lain dead for ten years. As my finger rested upon the little button that actuated the motor that was to send the revivifying liquid into those dormant veins, I experienced such a sensation as I imagine no mortal man has ever felt.

I had become master of life and death, and yet at this moment that I stood there upon the point of resurrecting the dead I felt more like a murderer than a saviour. I tried to view the procedure dispassionately through the cold eye of science, but I failed miserably. I could only see a stricken girl grieving for her lost beauties. With a muffled oath I turned away. I could not do it! And then, as though an outside force had seized upon me, my finger moved unerringly to the button and pressed it. I cannot explain it, unless upon the theory of dual mentality, which may explain many things. Perhaps my subjective mind directed the act. I do not know. Only I know that I did it, the motor started, the level of the blood in the container commenced gradually to lower.

Spellbound, I stood watching. Presently the vessel was empty. I shut off the motor, removed the tubes, sealed the openings with tape. The red glow of life tinged the body, replacing the sallow, purplish hue of death. The breasts rose and fell regularly, the head turned slightly and the eyelids moved. A faint sigh issued from between the parting lips. For a long time there was no other sign of life, then suddenly, the eyes opened. They were dull at first, but presently they commenced to fill with questioning wonderment. They rested on me and then passed on about that portion of the room that was visible from the position of the body. Then they came back to me and remained steadily fixed upon my countenance after having once surveyed me up and down. There was still the questioning in them, but there was no fear.

'Where am I?' she asked. The voice was that of an old woman—high and harsh. A startled expression filled her eyes. 'What is the matter with me? What is wrong with my voice? What has happened?'

I laid a hand upon her forehead. 'Don't bother about it now,' I said, soothingly. 'Wait until some time when you are stronger. Then I will tell you.'

She sat up. 'I am strong,' she said, and then her eyes swept her lower body and limbs and a look of utter horror crossed her face. 'What has happened to me? In the name of my first ancestor, what has happened to me?'

The shrill, harsh voice grated upon me. It was the voice of Xaxa and Xaxa must now possess the sweet musical tones that alone would have harmonized with the beautiful face she had stolen. I tried to forget those strident notes and think only of the pulchritude of the envelope that had once graced the soul within this old and withered carcass.

She extended a hand and laid it gently upon mine. The act was beautiful, the movements graceful. The brain of the girl directed the muscles, but the old, rough vocal chords of Xaxa could give forth no sweeter notes. 'Tell me, please!' she begged. There were tears in the old eyes, I'll venture for the first time in many years. 'Tell me! You do not seem unkind.'

And so I told her. She listened intently and when I was through she sighed. 'After all,' she said, 'it is not so dreadful, now that I really know. It is better than being dead.' That made me glad that I had pressed the button. She was glad to be alive, even draped in the hideous carcass of Xaxa. I told her as much.

'You were so beautiful,' I told her.

'And now I am so ugly?' I made no answer.

'After all, what difference does it make?' she inquired presently. 'This old body cannot change me, or make me different from what I have always been. The good in me remains and whatever of sweetness and kindness, and I can be happy to be alive and perhaps to do some good. I was terrified at first, because I did not know what had happened to me. I thought that maybe I had contracted some terrible disease that had so altered me—that horrified me; but now that I know—pouf! what of it?'

'You are wonderful,' I said. 'Most women would have gone mad with the horror and grief of it—to lose such wondrous beauty as was yours—and you do not care.'

'Oh, yes, I care, my friend,' she corrected me, 'but I do not care enough to ruin my life in all other respects because of it, or to cast a shadow upon the lives of those around me. I have had my beauty and enjoyed it. It is not an unalloyed happiness, I can assure you. Men killed one another because of it; two great nations went to war because of it; and perhaps my father lost his throne or his life—I do not know, for I was captured by the enemy while the war still raged. It may be raging yet and men dying because I was too beautiful. No one will fight for me now, though,' she added, with a rueful smile.

'Do you know how long you have been here?' I asked.

'Yes,' she replied. 'It was the day before yesterday that they brought me hither.'

'It was ten years ago,' I told her.

'Ten years! Impossible.'

I pointed to the corpses around us. 'You have lain like this for ten years,' I explained. 'There are subjects here who have lain thus for fifty, Ras Thavas tells me.'

'Ten years! Ten years! What may not have happened in ten years! It is better thus. I should fear to go back now. I should not want to know that my father, my mother too, perhaps, were gone. It is better thus. Perhaps you will let me sleep again? May I not?'

'That remains with Ras Thavas,' I replied; 'but for a while I am to observe you.'

'Observe me?'

'Study you—your reactions.'

'Ah! and what good will that do?'

'It may do some good in the world.'

'It may give this horrid Ras Thavas some new ideas for his torture chamber—some new scheme for coining money from the suffering of his victims,' she said, her harsh voice saddened.

'Some of his works are good,' I told her. 'The money he makes permits him to maintain this wonderful establishment where he constantly carries on countless experiments. Many of his operations are beneficent. Yesterday a warrior was brought in whose arm was crushed beyond repair. Ras Thavas gave him a new arm. A demented child was brought. Ras Thavas gave her a new brain. The arm and the brain were taken from two who had met violent deaths. Through Ras Thavas they were permitted, after death, to give life and happiness to others.'

She thought for a moment. 'I am content,' she said. 'I only hope that you will always be the observer.'

Presently Ras Thavas came and examined her. 'A good subject,' he said. He looked at the chart where I had made a very brief record following the other entries relative to the history of Case No. 4296-E-2631-H. Of course this is, naturally, a rather free translation of this particular identification number. The Barsoomians have no alphabet such as ours and their numbering system is quite different. The thirteen characters above were represented by four Toonolian characters, yet the meaning was quite the same—they represented, in contracted form, the case number, the room, the table and the building.

'The subject will be quartered near you where you may regularly observe it,' continued Ras Thavas. 'There is a chamber adjoining yours. I will see that it is unlocked. Take the subject there. When not under your observation, lock it in.' *It* was only another *case* to him.

I took the girl, if I may so call her, to her quarters. On the way I asked her her name, for it seemed to me an unnecessary discourtesy always to address her and refer to her as 4296-E-2631-H, and this I explained to her.

'It is considerate of you to think of that,' she said, 'but really that is all that I am here—just another subject for vivisection.'

'You are more than that to me,' I told her. 'You are friendless and helpless. I want to be of service to you—to make your lot easier if I can.'

'Thank you again,' she said. 'My name is Valla Dia, and yours?'

'Ras Thavas calls me Vad Varo,' I told her.

'But that is not your name?'

'My name is Ulysses Paxton.'

'It is a strange name, unlike any that I have ever heard, but you are unlike any man I have ever seen—you do not seem Barsoomian. Your colour is unlike that of any race.'

'I am not of Barsoom, but from Earth, the planet you sometimes call Jasoom. That is why I differ in appearance from any you have known before.'

'Jasoom! There is another Jasoomian here whose fame has reached to the remotest corners of Barsoom, but I never have seen him.'

'John Carter?' I asked.

'Yes, the War Lord. He was of Helium and my people were not friendly with those of Helium. I never could understand how he came here. And now there is another from Jasoom—how can it be? How did you cross the great void?'

I shook my head. 'I cannot even guess,' I told her.

'Jasoom must be peopled with wonderful men,' she said. It was a pretty compliment.

'As Barsoom is with beautiful women,' I replied.

She glanced down ruefully at her old and wrinkled body.

'I have seen the real you,' I said gently.

'I hate to think of my face,' she said. 'I know it is a frightful thing.'

'It is not you, remember that when you see it and do not feel too badly.'

'Is it as bad as that?' she asked.

I did not reply. 'Never mind,' she said presently. 'If I had not beauty of the soul, I was not beautiful, no matter how perfect my features may have been; but if I possessed beauty of soul then I have it now. So I can think beautiful thoughts and perform beautiful deeds and that, I think, is the real test of beauty, after all.'

'And there is hope,' I added, almost in a whisper.

'Hope? No, there is no hope, if what you mean to suggest is that I may some time regain my lost self. You have told me enough to convince me that that can never be.'

'We will not speak of it,' I said; 'but we may think of it and sometimes thinking a great deal of a thing helps us to find a way to get it, if we want it badly enough.'

'I do not want to hope,' she said, 'for it will but mean disappointment for me. I shall be happy as I am. Hoping, I should always be unhappy.'

I had ordered food for her and after it was brought Ras Thavas sent for me and I left her, locking the door of her chamber as the old surgeon had instructed. I found Ras Thavas in his office, a small room which adjoined a very large one in which were a score of clerks arranging and classifying reports from various departments of the great laboratory. He arose as I entered.

'Come with me, Vad Varo,' he directed. 'We will have a look at the two cases in L-42-X, the two of which I spoke.'

'The man with half a simian brain and the ape with a half human brain?' I asked.

He nodded and preceded me towards the runway that led to the vaults beneath the building. As we descended, the corridors and passageways indicated long disuse. The floors were covered with an impalpable dust, long undisturbed; the tiny radium bulbs that faintly illuminated the sub-Barsoomian depths were likewise coated. As we proceeded, we passed many doorways on either side, each marked with its descriptive hieroglyphic. Several of the openings had been tightly sealed with masonry. What gruesome secrets were hidden within? At last we came to L-42-X. Here the bodies were arranged on shelves, several rows of which almost completely filled the room from floor to ceiling, except for a rectangular space in the centre of the chamber, which accommodated an ersite topped operating table with its array of surgical instruments, its motor and other laboratory equipment.

Ras Thavas searched out the subjects of his strange experiment and together we carried the human body to the table. While Ras Thavas attached the tubes I returned for the vessel of blood which reposed upon the same shelf with the corpse. The now familiar method of revivification was soon accomplished and presently we were watching the return of consciousness to the subject.

The man sat up and looked at us, then he cast a quick glance about the chamber; there was a savage light in his eyes as they returned to us. Slowly he backed from the table to the floor, keeping the former between us.

'We will not harm you,' said Ras Thavas. The man attempted to reply, but his words were unintelligible gibberish, then he shook his head and growled. Ras Thavas took a step towards him and the man dropped to all fours, his knuckles resting on the floor, and backed away, growling.

'Come!' cried Ras Thavas. 'We will not harm you.' Again he attempted to approach the subject, but the man only backed quickly away, growling more fiercely; and then suddenly he wheeled and climbed quickly to the top of the highest shelf, where he squatted upon a corpse and gibbered at us.

'We shall have to have help,' said Ras Thavas and, going to the doorway, he blew a signal upon his whistle.

'What are you blowing that for?' demanded the man suddenly. 'Who are you? What am I doing here? What has happened to me?'

'Come down,' said Ras Thavas. 'We are friends.'

Slowly the man descended to the floor and came towards us, but he still moved with his knuckles to the pavement. He looked about at the corpses and a new light entered his eyes.

'I am hungry!' he cried. 'I will eat!' and with that he seized the nearest corpse and dragged it to the floor.

'Stop! Stop!' cried Ras Thavas, leaping forward. 'You will ruin the subject,' but the man only backed away, dragging the corpse along the floor after him. It was then that the attendants came and with their help we subdued and bound the poor creature. Then Ras Thavas had the attendants bring the body of the ape and he told them to remain, as we might need them.

The subject was a large specimen of the Barsoomian white ape, one of the most savage and fearsome denizens of the Red Planet, and because of the creature's great strength and ferocity Ras Thavas took the precaution to see that it was securely bound before resurgence.

It was a colossal creature about ten or fifteen feet tall, standing erect, and had an intermediary set of arms or legs midway between its upper and lower limbs. The eyes were close together and non-protruding; the ears were high set, while its snout and teeth were strikingly like those of our African gorilla.

With returning consciousness the creature eyed us questioningly. Several times it seemed to essay to speak, but only inarticulate sounds issued from its throat. Then it lay still for a period.

Ras Thavas spoke to it. 'If you understand my words, nod your head.' The creature nodded.

'Would you like to be freed of your bonds?' asked the surgeon.

Again the creature nodded an affirmative.

'I fear that you will attempt to injure us, or escape,' said Ras Thavas.

The ape was apparently trying very hard to articulate and at last there issued from its lips a sound that could not be misunderstood. It was the single word no.

'You will not harm us or try to escape?' Ras Thavas repeated his question.

'No,' said the ape, and this time the word was clearly enunciated.

'We shall see,' said Ras Thavas. 'But remember that with our weapons we may dispatch you quickly if you attack us.'

The ape nodded, and then, very laboriously 'I will not harm you.'

At a sign from Ras Thavas the attendants removed the bonds and the creature sat up. It stretched its limbs and slid easily to the floor, where it stood erect upon two feet, which was not surprising, since the white ape goes more often upon two feet than six; a fact of which I was not cognizant at the time, but which Ras Thavas explained to me later in commenting upon the fact that the human subject had gone upon all fours, which, to Ras Thavas, indicated a reversion to type in the fractional ape-brain transplanted to the human skull.

Ras Thavas examined the subject at considerable length and then resumed his examination of the human subject which continued to evince more simian characteristics than human, though it spoke more easily than the ape, because, undoubtedly, of its more perfect vocal organs. It was only by exerting the closest attention that the diction of the ape became understandable at all.

'There is nothing remarkable about these subjects,' said Ras Thavas, after devoting half a day to them. 'They bear out what I had already determined years ago in the transplanting of entire brains; that the act of transplanting stimulates growth and activity of brain cells. You will note that in each subject the transplanted portions of the brains are more active—they, in a considerable measure, control. That is why we have the human subject displaying distinctly simian characteristics, while the ape behaves in a more human manner; though if longer and closer observation were desirable you would doubtless find that each reverted at times to his own nature—that is, the ape would be more wholly an ape and the human more manlike—but it is not worth the time, of which I have already given too much to a rather unprofitable forenoon. I shall leave you now to restore the subjects to anaesthesia while I return to the laboratories above. The attendants will remain here to assist you, if required.'

The ape, who had been an interested listener, now stepped forward. 'Oh, please, I pray you,' it mumbled, 'do not again condemn me to these horrid shelves. I recall the day that I was brought here securely bound, and though I have no recollection of what has transpired since I can but guess from the appearance of my own skin and that of these dusty corpses that I have lain here long. I beg that you will permit me to live and either restore me to my fellows or allow me to serve in some capacity in this establishment, of which I saw something between the time of my capture and the day that I was carried into this laboratory, bound and helpless, to one of your cold, ersite slabs.'

Ras Thavas made a gesture of impatience. 'Nonsense!' he cried. 'You are better off here, where you can be preserved in the interests of science.'

'Accede to his request,' I begged, 'and I will myself take over all responsibility for him while I profit by the study that he will afford me.'

'Do as you are directed,' snapped Ras Thavas as he quit the room.

I shrugged my shoulders. 'There is nothing for it, then,' I said.

'I might dispatch you all and escape,' mused the ape, aloud, 'but you would have helped me. I could not kill one who would have befriended me—yet I shrink from the thought of another death. How long have I lain here?'

I referred to the history of his case that had been brought and suspended at the head of the table. 'Twelve years,' I told him.

'And yet, why not?' he demanded of himself. 'This man would slay me—why should I not slay him first.'

'It would do you no good,' I assured him, 'for you could never escape. Instead you would be really killed, dying a death from which Ras Thavas would probably think it not worth while ever to recall you, while I, who might find the opportunity at some later date and who have the inclination, would be dead at your hands and thus incapable of saving you.'

I had been speaking in a low voice, close to his ear, that the attendants might not overhear me. The ape listened intently.

'You will do as you suggest?' he asked.

'At the first opportunity that presents itself,' I assured him.

'Very well,' he said, 'I will submit, trusting to you.'

A half-hour later both subjects had been returned to their shelves.

THE COMPACT

DAYS ran into weeks, weeks into months, as day by day I laboured at the side of Ras Thavas, and more and more the old surgeon took me into his confidence, more and more he imparted to me the secrets of his skill and his profession. Gradually he permitted me to perform more and more important functions in the actual practice of his vast laboratory. I started transferring limbs from one subject to another, then internal organs of the digestive tract. Then he entrusted to me a complete operation upon a paying client. I removed the kidneys from a rich old man, replacing them with healthy ones from a young subject. The following day I gave a stunted child new thyroid glands. A week later I transferred two hearts and then, at last, came the great day for me—unassisted, with Ras Thavas standing silently beside me, I took the brain of an old man and transplanted it within the cranium of a youth.

When I had done Ras Thavas laid a hand upon my shoulder. 'I could not have done better myself,' he said. He seemed much elated and I could not but wonder at this unusual demonstration of emotion upon his part, he who so prided himself upon his lack of emotionalism. I had often pondered the purpose which influenced Ras Thavas to devote so much time to my training, but never had I hit upon any more satisfactory explanation than that he had need of assistance in his growing practice. Yet when I consulted the records, that were now open to me, I discovered that his practice was no greater than it had been for many years; and even had it been there was really no reason why he should have trained me in preference to one of his red-Martian assistants, his belief in my loyalty not being sufficient warrant, in my mind, for this preferment when he could, as well as not, have kept me for a bodyguard and trained one of his own kind to aid him in his surgical work.

But I was presently to learn that he had an excellent reason for what he was doing—Ras Thavas always had an excellent reason for whatever he did. One night after we had finished our evening meal he sat looking at me intently as he so often did, as though he would read my mind, which, by the way, he was totally unable to do, much to his surprise and chagrin; for unless a Martian is constantly upon the alert any other Martian can read clearly his every thought; but Ras Thavas was unable to read mine. He said that it was due to the fact that I was not a Barsoomian. Yet I could often read the minds of his assistants, when they were off their guard, though never had I read aught of Ras Thavas' thoughts, nor, I am sure, had any other read them. He kept his brain sealed like one of his own blood jars, nor was he ever for a moment found with his barriers down.

He sat looking at me this evening for a long time, nor did it in the least embarrass me, so accustomed was I to his peculiarities. 'Perhaps,' he said presently, 'one of the reasons that I trust you is due to the fact that I cannot ever, at any time, fathom your mind; so, if you harbour traitorous thoughts concerning me I do not know it, while the others, every one of them, reveal their inmost souls to my searching mind and in each one there is envy, jealousy or hatred of me. Them, I know, I cannot trust. Therefore I must accept the risk and place all my dependence upon you, and my reason tells me that my choice is a wise one—I have told you upon what grounds it based my selection of you as my bodyguard. The same holds true in my selection of you for the thing I have in mind. You cannot harm me without harming yourself and no man will intentionally do that; nor is there any reason why you should feel any deep antagonism towards me.

'You are, of course, a sentimentalist and doubtless you look with horror upon many of the acts of a sane, rational, scientific mind; but you are also highly intelligent and can, therefore, appreciate better than another, even though you may not approve them, the motives that prompt me to do many of those things of which your sentimentality disapproves. I may have offended you, but I have never wronged you, nor have I wronged any creature for which you might have felt some of your so-called friendship or love. Are my premises incorrect, or my reasoning faulty?'

I assured him to the contrary.

'Very well! Now let me explain why I have gone to such pains to train you as no other human being, aside from myself, has ever been trained. I am not ready to use you yet, or rather you are not ready; but if you know my purpose you will realize the necessity for bending your every energy to the consummation of my purpose, and to that end you will strive even more diligently than you have to perfect yourself in the high, scientific art I am imparting to you.

'I am a very old man,' he continued after a brief pause, 'even as age goes upon Barsoom. I have lived more than a thousand years. I have passed the allotted natural span of life, but I am not through with my life's work—I have but barely started it. I must not die. Barsoom must not be robbed of this wondrous brain and skill of mine. I have long had in mind a plan to thwart death, but it required another with skill equal to mine—two such might live for ever. I have selected you to be that other, for reasons that I already have explained—they are undefiled by sentimentalism. I did not choose you because I love you, or because I feel friendship for you, or because I think that you love me, or feel friendship towards me. I chose you because I knew that of all the inhabitants of a world you were the one least likely to fail me. For a time you will have my life in your hands. You will understand now why I have not been able to choose carelessly.

'This plan that I have chosen is simplicity itself provided that I can count upon just two essential factors—skill and self-interested loyalty in an assistant. My body is about worn out. I must have a new one. My laboratory is filled with wonderful bodies, young and complete with potential strength and health. I have but to select one of these and have my skilled assistant transfer my brain from this old carcass to the new one.' He paused.

'I understand now, why you have trained me,' I said. 'It has puzzled me greatly.'

'Thus and thus only may I continue my labours,' he went on, 'and thus may Barsoom be assured a continuance, practically indefinitely, of the benefits that my brain may bestow upon her children. I may live for ever, provided I always have a skilled assistant, and I may assure myself of such by seeing to it that he never dies; when he wears out one organ, or his whole body, I can replace either from my great storehouse of perfect parts, and for me he can perform the same service. Thus may we continue to live indefinitely; for the brain, I believe, is almost deathless, unless injured or attacked by disease.

'You are not ready as yet to be entrusted with this important task. You must transfer many more brains and meet with and overcome the various irregularities and idiosyncrasies that constitute the never failing differences that render no two operations identical. When you gain sufficient proficiency I shall be the first to know it and then we shall lose no time in making Barsoom safe for posterity.'

The old man was far from achieving hatred of himself. However, his plan was an excellent one, both for himself and for me. It assured us immortality—we might live forever and always with strong, healthy, young bodies. The outlook was alluring—and what a wonderful position it placed me in. If the old man could be assured of my loyalty because of self-interest, similarly might I depend upon his loyalty; for he could not afford to antagonize the one creature in the world who could assure him immortality, or withhold it from him. For the first time since I had entered his establishment I felt safe.

As soon as I had left him I went directly to Valla Dia's apartment, for I wanted to tell her this wonderful news. In the weeks that had passed since her resurrection I had seen much of her and in our daily intercourse there had been revealed to me little by little the wondrous beauties of her soul, until at last I no longer saw the hideous, disfigured face of Xaxa when I looked upon her, but the eyes of my heart penetrated deeper to the loveliness that lay within that sweet mind. She had become my confidant, as I was hers, and this association constituted the one great pleasure of my existence upon Barsoom.

Her congratulations, when I told her of what had come to me, were very sincere and lovely. She said that she hoped I would use this great power of mine to do good in the world. I assured her that I would and that among the first things that I should demand of Ras Thavas was that he should give Valla Dia a beautiful body; but she shook her head.

'No, my friend,' she said, 'if I may not have my own body this old one of Xaxa's is quite as good for me as another. Without my own body I should not care to return to my native country; while were Ras Thavas to give me the beautiful body of another, I should always be in danger of the covetousness of his clients, any one of whom might see and desire to purchase it, leaving to me her old husk, conceivably one quite terribly diseased or maimed. No, my friend, I am satisfied with the body of Xaxa, unless I may again possess my own, for Xaxa at least bequeathed me a tough and healthy envelope, however ugly it may be; and for what do looks count here? You, alone, are my friend—that I have your friendship is enough. You admire me for what I am, not for what I look like, so let us leave well enough alone.'

'If you could regain your own body and return to your native country, you would like that?' I demanded.

'Oh, do not say it!' she cried. 'The simple thought of it drives me mad with longing. I must not harbour so hopeless a dream that at best may only tantalize me into greater abhorrence of my lot.'

'Do not say that it is hopeless,' I urged. 'Death, only, renders hope futile.'

'You mean to be kind,' she said, 'but you are only hurting me. There can be no hope.'

'May I hope for you, then?' I asked. 'For I surely see a way; however slight a possibility for success it may have, still, it is a way.'

She shook her head. 'There is no way,' she said, with finality. 'No more will Duhor know me.'

'Duhor?' I repeated. 'Your—someone you care for very much?'

'I care for Duhor very much,' she answered with a smile, 'but Duhor is not someone—Duhor is my home, the country of my ancestors.'

'How came you to leave Duhor?' I asked. 'You have never told me, Valla Dia.'

'It was because of the ruthlessness of Jal Had, Prince of Amhor,' she replied. 'Hereditary enemies were Duhor and Amhor; but Jal Had came disguised into the city of Duhor, having heard, they say, of the great beauty attributed to the only daughter of Kor San, Jeddak of Duhor; and when he had seen her he determined to possess her. Returning to Amhor he sent ambassadors to the court of Kor San to sue for the hand of the Princess of Duhor; but Kor San, who had no son, had determined to wed his daughter to one of his own Jeds, that the son of this union, with the blood of Kor San in his veins, might rule over the people of Duhor; and so the offer of Jal Had was declined.

'This so incensed the Amhorian that he equipped a great fleet and set forth to conquer Duhor and take by force that which he could not win by honourable methods. Duhor was, at that time, at war with Helium and all her forces were far afield in the south, with the exception of a small army that had been left behind to guard the city. Jal Had. therefore, could not have selected a more propitious time for an attack. Duhor fell, and while his troops were looting the fair city Jal Had, with a picked force, sacked the palace of the jeddak and searched for the princess; but the princess had no mind to go back with him as Princess of Amhor. From the moment that the vanguard of the Amhorian fleet was seen in the sky she had known, with the others of the city, the purpose for which they came and so she used her head to defeat that purpose.

'There was in her retinue a cosmetologist whose duty it was to preserve the lustrous beauty of the princess's hair and skin and prepare her for public audiences, for fêtes and for the daily intercourse of the court. He was a master of his art; he could render the ugly pleasant to look upon, he could make the plain lovely, and he could make the lovely radiant. She called him quickly to her and commanded him to make the radiant ugly; and when he had done with her none might guess that she was the Princess of Duhor, so deftly had he wrought with his pigments and his tiny brushes.

'When Jal Had could not find the princess within the palace, and no amount of threat or torture could force a statement of her whereabouts from the loyal lips of her people, the Amhorian ordered that every woman within the palace be seized and taken to Amhor; there to be held as hostages until the princess of Duhor should be delivered to him in marriage. We were, therefore, all seized and placed upon an Amhorian war ship which was sent back to Amhor ahead of the balance of the fleet, which remained to complete the sacking of Duhor.

'When the ship, with its small convoy, had covered some four thousand of the five thousand haads that separate Duhor from Amhor, it was sighted by a fleet from Phundahl which immediately attacked. The convoying ships were destroyed or driven off and that which carried us was captured. We were taken to Phundahl where we were put upon the auction block and I fell to the bid of one of Ras Thavas' agents. The rest you know.'

'And what became of the princess?' I asked.

'Perhaps she died—her party was separated in Phundahl—but death could not more definitely prevent her return to Duhor. The Princess of Duhor will never again see her native country.'

'But you may!' I cried, for I had suddenly hit upon a plan. 'Where is Duhor?'

'You are going there?' she asked, laughingly.

'Yes!'

'You are mad, my friend,' she said. 'Duhor lies a full seven thousand, eight hundred haads from Toonol, upon the opposite side of the snow-clad Artolian Hills. You, a stranger and alone, could never reach it; for between lie the Toonolian Marshes, wild hordes, savage beasts and warlike cities. You would but die uselessly within the first dozen haads, even could you escape from the island upon which stands the laboratory of Ras Thavas; and what motive is there to prompt you to such a useless sacrifice?'

I could not tell her. I could not look upon that withered figure and into that hideous and disfigured face and say: 'It is because I love you, Valla Dia.' But that, alas, was my only reason. Gradually, as I had come to know her through the slow revealment of the wondrous beauty of her mind and soul, there had crept into my heart a knowledge of my love; and yet, explain it I cannot, I could not speak the words to that frightful old hag. I had seen the gorgeous mundane tabernacle that had housed the equally gorgeous spirit of the real Valla Dia—*that* I could love; her heart and soul and mind I could love; but I could not love the body of Xaxa. I was torn, too, by other emotions, induced by a great doubt—could Valla Dia return my love. Habilitated in the corpse of Xaxa, with no other suitor, nay, with no other friend, she might, out of gratitude or through sheer loneliness, be attracted to me; but once again were she Valla Dia the beautiful and returned to the palace of her king surrounded by the great nobles of Duhor, would she have either eyes or heart for a lone and friendless exile from another world? I doubted it—and yet that doubt did not deter me from my determination to carry out, as far as Fate would permit, the mad scheme that was revolving in my brain.

'You have not answered my question, Vad Varo,' she interrupted my surging thoughts. 'Why would you do this thing?'

'To right the wrong that has been done you, Valla Dia,' I said.

She sighed. 'Do not attempt it, please,' she begged. 'You would but rob me of my one friend, whose association is the only source of happiness remaining to me. I appreciate your generosity and your loyality, even though I may not understand them; your unselfish desire to serve me at such suicidal risk touches me more deeply than I can reveal, adding still further to the debt I owe you; but you must not attempt it—you must not.'

'If it troubles you, Valla Dia,' I replied 'we will not speak of it again; but know always that it is never from my thoughts. Some day I shall find a way, even though the plan I now have fails me.'

The days moved on and on, the gorgeous Martian nights, filled with her hurtling moons, followed one upon another. Ras Thavas spent more and more time in directing my work of brain transference. I had long since become an adept; and I realized that the time was rapidly approaching when Ras Thavas would feel that he could safely entrust to my hands and skill his life and future. He would be wholly within my power and he knew that I knew it. I could slay him; I could permit him to remain for ever in the preserving grip of his own anaesthetic; or I could play any trick upon him that I chose, even to giving him the body of a calot or a part of the brain of an ape; but he must take the chance and that I knew, for he was failing rapidly. Already almost stone blind, it was only the wonderful spectacles that he had himself invented that permitted him to see at all; long deaf, he used artificial means for hearing; and now his heart was showing symptoms of fatigue that he could no longer ignore.

One morning I was summoned to his sleeping apartment by a slave. I found the old surgeon lying, a shrunken, pitiful heap of withered skin and bones.

'We must hasten, Vad Varo,' he said in a weak whisper. 'My heart was like to have stopped a few tals ago. It was then that I sent for you.' He pointed to a door leading from his chamber. 'There,' he said, 'you will find the body I have chosen. There, in the private laboratory I long ago built for this very purpose, you will perform the greatest surgical operation that the universe has ever known, transferring its most perfect brain to the most beautiful and perfect body that ever has passed beneath these ancient eyes. You will find the head already prepared to receive my brain; the brain of the subject having been removed and destroyed—totally destroyed by fire. I could not possibly chance the existence of a brain desiring and scheming to regain its wondrous body. No, I destroyed it. Call slaves and have them bear my body to the ersite slab.'

'That will not be necessary,' I told him; and lifting his shrunken form in my arms as he had been an earthly babe, I carried him into the adjoining room where I found a perfectly lighted and appointed laboratory containing two operating tables, one of which was occupied by the body of a red-man. Upon the surface of the other, which was vacant, I laid Ras Thavas, then I turned to look at the new envelope he had chosen. Never, I believe, had I beheld so perfect a form, so handsome a face—Ras Thavas had indeed chosen well for himself. Then I turned back to the old surgeon. Deftly, as he had taught me, I made the two incisions and attached the tubes. My finger rested upon the button that would start the motor pumping his blood from his veins and his marvellous preservative-anaesthetic into them. Then I spoke.

'Ras Thavas,' I said, 'you have long been training me to this end. I have laboured assiduously to prepare myself that there might be no slightest cause for apprehension as to the outcome. You have, coincidentally, taught me that one's every act should be prompted by self-interest only. You are satisfied, therefore, that I am not doing this for you because I love you, or because I feel any friendship for you; but you think that you have offered me enough in placing before me a similar opportunity for immortality.

'Regardless of your teaching I am afraid that I am still

somewhat of a sentimentalist. I crave the redressing of wrongs. I crave friendship and love. The price you offer is not enough. Are you willing to pay more that this operation may be successfully concluded?'

He looked at me steadily for a long minute. 'What do you want?' he asked. I could see that he was trembling with anger, but he did not raise his voice.

'Do you recall 4296-E-2631-H?' I inquired.

'The subject with the body of Xaxa? Yes, I recall the case. What of it?'

'I wish her body returned to her. That is the price you must pay for this operation.'

He glared at me. 'It is impossible. Xaxa has the body. Even if I dared to do so, I could never recover it. Proceed with the operation!'

'When you have promised me,' I insisted.

'I cannot promise the impossible—I cannot obtain Xaxa. Ask me something else. I am not unwilling to grant any reasonable request.'

'That is all I wish—just that; but I do not insist that you obtain the body. If I bring Xaxa here will you make the transfer?'

'It would mean war between Toonol and Phundahl,' he fumed.

'That does not interest me,' I said. 'Quick! Reach a decision. In five tals I shall press this button. If you promise what I ask, you shall be restored with a new and beautiful body; if you refuse you shall lie here in the semblance of death for ever.'

'I promise,' he said slowly, 'that when you bring the body of Xaxa to me I will transfer to that body any brain that you select from among my subjects.'

'Good!' I exclaimed, and pressed the button.

DANGER

Ras Thavas awakened from the anaesthetic a new and gorgeous creature—a youth of such wondrous beauty that he seemed of heavenly rather than worldly origin; but in that beautiful head was the hard, cold, thousand-year-old brain of the master surgeon. As he opened his eyes he looked upon me coldly.

'You have done well,' he said.

'What I have done, I have done for friendship—perhaps for love,' I said, 'so you can thank the sentimentalism you decry for the success of the transfer.'

He made no reply.

'And now,' I continued, 'I shall look to you for the fulfillment of the promise you have made me.'

'When you bring Xaxa's body I shall transfer to it the brain of any of my subjects you may select,' he said, 'but were I you, I would not risk my life in such an impossible venture—you cannot succeed. Select another body—there are many beautiful ones—and I will give it the brain of 4296-E-2631-H.'

'None other than the body now owned by the Jeddara Xaxa will fulfil your promise to me,' I said.

He shrugged and there was a cold smile upon his handsome lips. 'Very well,' he said, 'fetch Xaxa. When do you start?'

'I am not yet ready. I will let you know when I am.'

'Good and now begone—but wait! First go to the office and see what cases await us and if there be any that do not require my personal attention, and they fall within your skill and knowledge, attend to them yourself.'

As I left him I noticed a crafty smile of satisfaction upon his lips. What had aroused that? I did not like it and as I walked away I tried to conjure what could possibly have passed through that wondrous brain to call forth at that particular instant so unpleasant a smile. As I passed through the doorway and into the corridor beyond I heard him summon his personal slave and body servant, Yamdor, a huge fellow whose loyalty he kept through the bestowal of lavish gifts and countless favours. So great was the fellow's power that all feared him, as a word to the master from the lips of Yamdor might easily send any of the numerous slaves or attendants to an ersite slab for eternity. It was rumoured that he was the result of an unnatural experiment which had combined the brain of a woman with the body of a man, and there was much in his actions and mannerisms to justify this general belief. His touch, when he worked about his master, was soft and light, his movements graceful, his ways gentle, but his mind was jealous, vindictive and unforgiving.

I believed that he did not like me, through jealousy of the authority I had attained in the establishment of Ras Thavas; for there was no questioning the fact that I was a lieutenant, while he was but a slave; yet he always accorded me the utmost respect. He was, however, merely a minor cog in the machinery of the great institution presided over by the sovereign mind of Ras Thavas, and as such I had given him little consideration; nor did I now as I bent my steps towards the office.

I had gone but a short distance when I recalled a matter of importance upon which it was necessary for me to obtain instructions from Ras Thavas immediately; and so I wheeled about and retraced my way towards his apartments, through the open doorway of which, as I approached, I heard the new voice of the master surgeon. Ras Thavas had always spoken in rather loud tones, whether as a vocal reflection of his naturally domineering and authoritative character, or because of his deafness, I do not know; and now, with the fresh young vocal chords of his new body, his words rang out clearly and distinctly in the corridor leading to his room.

'You will, therefore, Yamdor,' he was saying, 'go at once

and, selecting two slaves in whose silence and discretion you may trust, take the subject from the apartments of Vad Varo and destroy it—let no vestige of body or brain remain. Immediately after, you will bring the two slaves to the laboratory F-30-L, permitting them to speak to no one, and I will consign them to silence and forgetfulness for eternity.

'Vad Varo will discover the absence of the subject and report the matter to me. During my investigation you will confess that you aided 4296-E-2631-H to escape, but that you have no idea where it intended going. I will sentence you to death as punishment, but at last, explaining how urgently I need your services and upon your solemn promise never to transgress again, I will defer punishment for the term of your continued good behaviour. Do you thoroughly understand the entire plan?'

'Yes, master,' replied Yamdor.

'Then depart at once and select the slaves who are to assist you.'

Quickly and silently I sped along the corridor until the first intersection permitted me to place myself out of sight of anyone coming from Ras Thavas' apartment; then I went directly to the chamber occupied by Valla Dia. Unlocking the door I threw it open and beckoned her to come out. 'Quick! Valla Dia!' I cried. 'No time is to be lost. In attempting to save you I have but brought destruction upon you. First we must find a hiding place for you, and that at once—afterwards we can plan for the future.'

The place that first occurred to me as affording adequate concealment was the half forgotten vaults in the pits beneath the laboratories, and towards these I hastened Valla Dia. As we proceeded I narrated all that had transpired, nor did she once reproach me; but, instead, expressed naught but gratitude for what she was pleased to designate as my unselfish friendship. That it had miscarried, she assured me, was no reflection upon me and she insisted that she would rather die in the knowledge that she possessed one such friend than to live on indefinitely, friendless.

We came at last to the chamber I sought—vault L-42-X, in building 4-J-21, where reposed the bodies of the ape and the man, each of which possessed half the brain of the other. Here I was forced to leave Valla Dia for the time, that I might hasten to the office and perform the duties imposed upon me by Ras Thavas, lest his suspicions be aroused when Yamdor reported that he had found her apartment vacant.

I reached the office without it being discovered by anyone who might report the fact to Ras Thavas that I had been a long time coming from his apartment. To my relief, I found there were no cases. Without appearing in any undue haste, I nevertheless soon found an excuse to depart and at once made my way towards my own quarters, moving in a leisurely and unconcerned manner and humming, as was my wont (a habit which greatly irritated Ras Thavas), snatches from some song that had been popular at the time that I quit Earth. In this instance it was 'Oh, Frenchy.'

I was thus engaged when I met Yamdor moving hurriedly along the corridor leading from my apartment, in company with two male slaves. I greeted him pleasantly, as was my custom, and he returned my greeting; but there was an expression of fear and suspicion in his eyes. I went at once to my quarters, opened the door leading to the chamber formerly occupied by Valla Dia and then hastened immediately to the apartment of Ras Thavas, where I found him conversing with Yamdor. I rushed in apparently breathless and simulating great excitement.

'Ras Thavas,' I demanded, 'what have you done with 4296-E-2631-H? She has disappeared; her apartment is empty; and as I was approaching it I met Yamdor and two other slaves coming from that direction.' I turned then upon Yamdor and pointed an accusing finger at him. 'Yamdor!' I cried. 'What have you done with this woman?'

Both Ras Thavas and Yamdor seemed genuinely puzzled and I congratulated myself that I had thus readily thrown them off the track. The master surgeon declared that he would make an immediate investigation; and he at once ordered a thorough search of the grounds and of the island outside the enclosure. Yamdor denied any knowledge of the woman and I, at least, was aware of the sincerity of his protestations, but not so Ras Thavas. I could see a hint of suspicion in his eyes as he questioned his body servant; but evidently he could conjure no motive for any such treasonable action on the part of Yamdor as would have been represented by the abduction of the woman and the consequent gross disobedience of orders.

Ras Thavas's investigation revealed nothing. I think as it progressed that he became gradually more and more imbued with a growing suspicion that I might know more about the disappearance of Valla Dia than my attitude indicated, for I presently became aware of a delicately concealed espionage. Up to this time I had been able to smuggle food to Valla Dia every night, after Ras Thavas had retired to his quarters. Then, on one occasion, I suddenly became subconsciously aware that I was being followed, and instead of going to the vaults I went to the office, where I added some observations to my report upon a case I had handled that day. Returning to my room I hummed a few bars from 'Over There', that the suggestion of my unconcern might be accentuated. From the moment that I quit my quarters until I returned to them I was sure that eyes had been watching my every move. What was I to do? Valla Dia must have food, without it she would die; and were I to be followed to her hiding place while taking it to her, she would die; Ras Thavas would see to that.

Half the night I lay awake, racking my brains for some solution to the problem. There seemed only one way—I must elude the spies. If I could do this but one single time I could carry out the balance of a plan that had occurred to me, and which was, I thought, the only one feasible that might eventually lead to the resurrection of Valla Dia in her own body. The way was long, the risks great; but I was young, in love and utterly reckless of consequences in so far as they concerned me; it was Valla Dia's happiness alone that I could not risk too greatly, other than under dire stress. Well, the stress existed and I must risk that, even as I risked my life.

My plan was formulated and I lay awake upon my sleeping silks and furs in the darkness of my room, awaiting the time when I might put it into execution. My window, which was upon the third floor, overlooked the walled enclosure, upon the scarlet sward of which I had made my first bow to Barsoom. Across the open casement I had watched Cluros, the farther moon, take his slow deliberate way. He had already set. Behind him, Thuria, his elusive mistress, fled through the heavens. In five xats (about 15 minutes) she would set; and then for about three and three-quarter Earth hours the heavens would be dark, except for the stars.

In the corridor, perhaps, lurked those watchful eyes. I prayed God that they might not be elsewhere as Thuria sank at last beneath the horizon and I swung to my window ledge, in my hand a long rope fabricated from braided strips torn from my sleeping silks while I had awaited the setting of the moons. One end I had fastened to a heavy sorapus bench which I had drawn close to the window. I dropped the free end of the rope and started my descent. My Earthly muscles, untried in such endeavours, I had not trusted to the task of carrying me to my window ledge in a single leap, when I should be returning. I felt that they would, but I did not know; and too much depended upon the success of my venture to risk any unnecessary chance of failure. And so I had prepared the rope.

Whether I was being observed I did not know. I must go on as though none were spying upon me. In less than four hours Thuria would return (just before the sudden Barsoomian dawn) and in the interval I must reach Valla Dia, persuade her of the necessity of my plan and carry out its details, returning to my chamber before Thuria could disclose me to any accidental observer. I carried my weapons with me and in my heart was unbending determination to slay whoever might cross my path and recognize me during the course of my errand, however innocent of evil intent against me he might be.

The night was quiet except for the usual distant sounds that I had heard ever since I had been here—sounds that I had interpreted as the cries of savage beasts. Once I had asked Ras Thavas about them, but he had been in ill humour and had ignored my question. I reached the ground quickly and without hesitation moved directly to the nearest entrance of the building, having previously searched out and determined upon the route I would follow to the vault. No one was visible and I was confident, when at last I reached the doorway, that I had come through undetected. Valla Dia was so happy to see me again that it almost brought the tears to my eyes.

'I thought that something had happened to you,' she cried, 'for I knew that you would not remain away so long of your own volition.'

I told her of my conviction that I was being watched and that it would not be possible for me longer to bring food to her without incurring almost certain detection, which would spell immediate death for her.

'There is a single alternative,' I said, 'and that I dread even to suggest and would not were there any other way. You must be securely hidden for a long time, until Ras Thavas' suspicions have been allayed; for as long as he has me watched I cannot possibly carry out the plans I have formulated for your eventual release, the restoration of your own body and your return to Duhor.'

'Your will shall be my law, Vad Varo.'

I shook my head. 'It will be harder for you than you imagine.'

'What is the way?' she asked.

I pointed to the ersite topped table. 'You must pass again through that ordeal that I may hide you away in this vault until the time is ripe for the carrying out of my plans. Can you endure it?'

She smiled. 'Why not?' she asked. 'It is only sleep—if it lasts for ever I shall be no wiser.'

I was surprised that she did not shrink from the idea, but I was very glad since I knew that it was the only way that we had a chance for success. Without my help she disposed herself upon the ersite slab.

'I am ready, Vad Varo,' she said, bravely; 'but first promise me that you will take no risks in this mad venture. You cannot succeed. When I close my eyes I know that it will be for the last time if my resurrection depends upon the successful outcome of the maddest venture that ever man conceived; yet I am happy, because I know that it is inspired by the greatest friendship with which any mortal woman has ever been blessed.'

As she talked I had been adjusting the tubes and now I stood beside her with my finger upon the starting button of the motor.

'Good-bye, Vad Varo' she whispered.

'Not good-bye, Valla Dia, but only a sweet sleep for what to you will be the briefest instant. You will seem but to close your eyes and open them again. As you see me now, I shall be standing here beside you as though I never had departed from you. As I am the last that you look upon tonight before you close your eyes, so shall I be the first that you shall look upon as you open them on that new and beautiful morning; but you shall not again look forth through the eyes of Xaxa, but from the limpid depths of your own beautiful orbs.'

She smiled and shook her head. Two tears formed beneath her lids. I pressed her hand in mine and touched the button.

SUSPICIONS

In so far as I could know I reached my apartment without detection. Hiding my rope where I was sure it would not be discovered, I sought my sleeping silks and furs and was soon asleep.

The following morning as I emerged from my quarters I caught a fleeting glimpse of a figure in a nearby corridor and from then on for a long time I had further evidence that Ras Thavas suspicioned me. I went at once to his quarters, as had been my habit. He seemed restless, but he gave me no hint that he held any assurance that I had been responsible for the disappearance of Valla Dia, and I think that he was far from positive of it. It was simply that his judgement pointed to the fact that I was the only person who might have any reason for interfering in any way with this particular subject, and he was having me watched to either prove or disprove the truth of his reasonable suspicions. His restlessness he explained to me himself.

'I have often studied the reaction of others who have undergone brain transference,' he said, 'and so I am not wholly surprised at my own. Not only has my brain energy been stimulated, resulting in an increased production of nervous energy, but I also feel the effects of the young tissue and youthful blood of my new body. They are affecting my consciousness in a way that my experiments had vaguely indicated, but which I now see must be actually experienced to be fully understood. My thoughts, my inclinations, even my ambitions have been changed, or at least coloured, by the transfer. It will take some time for me to find myself.'

Though uninterested, I listened politely until he was

through and then I changed the subject. 'Have you located the missing woman?' I asked.

He shook his head, negatively.

'You must appreciate, Ras Thavas,' I said, 'that I fully realize that you must have known that the removal or destruction of that woman would entirely frustrate my entire plan. You are master here. Nothing that passes is without your knowledge.'

'You mean that I am responsible for the disappearance of that woman?' he demanded.

'Certainly. It is obvious. I demand that she be restored.'

He lost his temper. 'Who are you to demand?' he shouted. 'You are naught but a slave. Cease your impudence or I shall erase you—erase you. It will be as though you never had existed.'

I laughed in his face. 'Anger is the most futile attribute of the sentimentalist,' I reminded him. 'You will not erase me, for I alone stand between you and mortality.'

'I can train another,' he parried.

'But you could not trust him,' I pointed out.

'But you bargained with me for my life when you had me in your power,' he cried.

'For nothing that it would have harmed you to have granted willingly. I did not ask anything for myself. Be that as it may, you will trust me again. You will trust, for no other reason than that you will be forced to trust me. So why not win my gratitude and my loyalty by returning the woman to me and carrying out in spirit as well as in fact the terms of our agreement?'

He turned and looked steadily at me. 'Vad Varo,' he said, 'I give you the word of honour of a Barsoomian noble that I know absolutely nothing concerning the whereabouts of 4296-E-2631-H.'

'Perhaps Yamdor does,' I persisted.

'Nor Yamdor. Of my knowledge no person in any way connected with me knows what became of it. I have spoken the truth.'

Well, the conversation was not as profitless as it might appear, for I was sure that it had almost convinced Ras Thavas that I was equally as ignorant of the fate of Valla Dia as was he. That it had not wholly convinced him was evidenced by the fact that the espionage continued for a long time, a fact which determined me to use Ras Thavas' own methods in my own defence. I had had allotted to me a number of slaves and these I had won over by kindness and understanding until I knew that I had the full measure of their loyalty. They had no reason to love Ras Thavas and every reason to hate him; on the other hand they had no reason to hate me, and I saw to it that they had every reason to love me.

The result was that I had no difficulty in enlisting the services of a couple of them to spy upon Ras Thavas' spies, with the result that I was soon apprised that my suspicions were well founded—I was being constantly watched every minute that I was out of my apartments, but the spying did not come beyond my outer chamber walls. That was why I had been successful in reaching the vault in the manner that I had; the spies, having assumed that I would leave my chamber only by its natural exit, had been content to guard that and permit my windows to go unwatched.

I think it was about two of our months that the spying continued and then my men reported that it seemed to have ceased entirely. All that time I was fretting at the delay, for I wanted to be about my plans,which would have been absolutely impossible for me to carry out if I were being watched. I had spent the interval in studying the geography of the north-eastern Barsoomian hemisphere where my activities were to be carried on, and also in scanning a great number of case histories and inspecting the subjects to which they referred but at last, with the removal of the spies, it began to look as though I might soon commence to put my plans in active operation.

Ras Thavas had for some time permitted me considerable freedom in independent investigation and experiment, and this I determined to take advantage of in every possible way that might put forward my plans for the resurrection of Valla Dia. My study of the histories of many of the cases had been with the possibility in mind of discovering subjects that might be of assistance to me in my venture. Among those that had occupied my careful attention were, quite naturally, the cases with which I had been most familiar. namely: 378-J-493811-P, the red-man from whose vicious attack I had saved Ras Thavas upon the day of my advent upon Mars and he whose brain had been divided with an ape.

The former, 378-J-493811-P, had been a native of Phundahl—a young warrior attached to the court of Xaxa, Jeddara of Phundahl—and a victim of assassination. His body had been purchased by a Phundahlian noble for the purpose, as Ras Thavas had narrated, of winning the favour of a young beauty. I felt that I might possibly enlist his services, but that would depend upon the extent of his loyalty towards Xaxa, which I could only determine by reviving and questioning him.

He whose brain had been divided with an ape had originated in Ptarth, which lay at a considerable distance to the west of Phundahl and a little south and about an equal distance from Duhor, which lay north and a little west of it. An inhabitant of Ptarth, I reasoned, would know much of the entire country included in the triangle formed by Phundahl, Ptarth and Duhor; the strength and ferocity of the great ape would prove of value in crossing beast infested wastes; and I felt that I could hold forth sufficient promise to the human half of the great beast's brain, which really now dominated the creature, to win its support and loyalty. The third subject that I had tentatively selected had been a notorious Toonolian assassin, whose audacity, fearlessness and swordsmanship had won for him a reputation that had spread far beyond the boundaries of his country.

Ras Thavas, himself a Toonolian, had given me something of the history of this man whose grim calling is not without honour upon Barsoom, and which Gor Hajus had raised still higher in the esteem of his countrymen through the fact that he never struck down a woman or a good man and that he never struck from behind. His killings were always the results of fair fights in which the victim had every opportunity to defend himself and slay his attacker; and he was famous for his loyalty to his friends. In fact this very loyalty had been a contributing factor in his downfall which had brought him to one of Ras Thavas' ersite slabs some years since, for he had earned the enmity of Vobis Kan, Jeddak of Toonol, through his refusal to assassinate a man who once had befriended Gor Hajus in some slight degree; following which Vobis Kan conceived the suspicion that Gor Hajus had him marked for slaying. The result was inevitable: Gor Hajus was arrested and condemned to death; immediately following the execution of the sentence an agent of Ras Thavas had purchased the body.

These three, then, I had chosen to be my partners in my great adventure. It is true that I had not discussed the matter with any one of them, but my judgement assured me that I would have no difficulty in enlisting their services and loyalty in return for their total resurrection.

My first task lay in renewing the organs of 378-J-4938-P and of Gor Hajus which had been injured by the wounds that had layed them low; the former requiring a new lung and the latter a new heart, his executioner having run him through with a short-sword. I hesitated to ask Ras Thavas's permission to experiment on these subjects for fear of the possibility of arousing his suspicions, in which event he would probably have them destroyed and so I was forced to accomplish my designs by subterfuge and stealth. To this end I made it a practice for weeks to carry my regular laboratory work far into the night, often requiring the services of various assistants that all might become accustomed to the sight of me at work at unusual hours. In my selection of these assistants I made it a point to choose two of the very spies that Ras Thavas had set to watching me. While it was true that they were no longer employed in this particular service, I had hopes that they would carry word of my activities to their master; and I was careful to see that they received from me the proper suggestions that would mould their report in language far from harmful to me. By the merest suggestion I carried to them the idea that I worked thus late purely for the love of the work itself and the tremendous interest in it that Ras Thavas had awakened within my mind. Some nights I worked with assistants and as often I did not, but always I was careful to assure myself that the following morning those in the office were made aware that I had laboured far into the preceding night.

This groundwork carefully prepared, I had comparatively little fear of the results of actual discovery when I set to work upon the warrior of Phundahl and the assassin of Toonol. I chose the former first. His lung was badly injured where my blade had passed through it, but from the laboratory where were kept fractional bodies I brought a perfect lung, with which I replaced the one that I had ruined. The work occupied but half the night. So anxious was I to complete my task that I immediately opened up the breast of Gor Hajus, for whom I had selected an unusually strong and powerful heart, and by working rapidly I succeeded in completing the transference before dawn. Having known the nature of the wounds that had dispatched these two men, I had spent weeks in performing similar operations that I might perfect myself especially in this work; and having encountered no unusual pathological conditions in either subject, the work had progressed smoothly and with great rapidity. I had completed what I had feared would be the most difficult part of my task and now, having removed as far as possible all signs of the operation except the therapeutic tape which closed the incisions, I returned to my quarters for a few minutes of much needed rest, praying that Ras Thavas would not by any chance examine either of the subjects upon which I had been working; although I had fortified myself against such a contingency by entering full details of the operation upon the history card of each subject that, in the event of discovery, any suspicion of ulterior motives upon my part might be allayed by my play of open frankness.

I arose at the usual time and went at once to Ras Thavas' apartment, where I was met with a bomb-shell that nearly wrecked my composure. He eyed me closely for a long minute before he spoke.

'You worked late last night, Vad Varo,' he said.

'I often do,' I replied, lightly; but my heart was heavy as a stone.

'And what might it have been that so occupied your interest?' he inquired.

I felt as a mouse with which the cat is playing. 'I have been doing quite a little lung and heart transference of late,' I replied, 'and I became so engrossed with my work that I did not note the passage of time.'

'I have known that you worked late at night. Do you think it wise?'

At that moment I felt that it had been very unwise, yet I assured him to the contrary.

'I was restless,' he said. 'I could not sleep and so I went to your quarters after midnight, but you were not there. I wanted someone with whom to talk, but your slaves knew only that you were not there—where you were they did not know—so I set out to search for you.' My heart went into my sandals. 'I guessed that you were in one of the laboratories, but though I visited several I did not find you.'

My heart arose with the lightness of a feather. 'Since my own transference I have been cursed with restlessness and sleeplessness, so that I could almost wish for the return of my old corse—the youth of my body harmonizes not with the antiquity of my brain. It is filled with latent urges and desires that comport illy with the serious subject matter of my mind.'

'What your body needs,' I said, 'is exercise. It is young, strong, virile. Work it hard and it will let your brain rest at night.'

'I know that you are right,' he replied. 'I have reached that same conclusion myself. In fact, not finding you, I walked in the gardens for an hour or more before returning to my quarters, and then I slept soundly. I shall walk every night when I cannot sleep, or I shall go into the laboratories and work as do you.'

This news was most disquieting. Now I could never be sure but that Ras Thavas was wandering about at night and I had one more very important night's work to do, perhaps two. The only way that I could be sure of him was to be with him.

'Send for me when you are restless,' I said, 'and I will walk and work with you. You should not go about thus at night alone.'

'Very well,' he said, 'I may do that occasionally.'

I hoped that he would do it always, for then I would know that when he failed to send for me he was safe in his own quarters. Yet I saw that I must henceforth face the menace of detection; and knowing this I determined to hasten the completion of my plans and to risk everything on a single bold stroke.

That night I had no opportunity to put it into action as Ras Thavas sent for me early and informed me that we would walk in the gardens until he was tired. Now, as I needed a full night for what I had in mind and as Ras Thavas walked until midnight, I was compelled to forgo everything for that evening, but the following morning I persuaded him to walk early on the pretext that I should like to go beyond the enclosure and see something of Barsoom beside the inside of his laboratories and his gardens. I had little confidence that he would grant my request, yet he did so. I am sure he never would have done it had he possessed his old body; but thus greatly had young blood changed Ras Thavas.

I had never been beyond the buildings, nor had I seen beyond, since there were no windows in the outside walls of any of the structures and upon the garden side the trees had grown to such a height that they obstructed all view beyond them. For a time we walked in another garden just inside the outer wall, and then I asked Ras Thavas if I might go even beyond this.

'No,' he said. 'It would not be safe.'

'And why not?' I asked.

'I will show you and at the same time give you a much broader view of the outside world than you could obtain by merely passing through the gate. Come, follow me!'

He led me immediately to a lofty tower that rose at the corner of the largest building of the group that comprised his vast establishment. Within was a circular runway which led not only upward, but down as well. This we ascended, passing openings at each floor, until we came at last out upon its lofty summit. About me spread the first Barsoomian landscape of any extent upon which my eyes had yet rested during the long months that I had spent upon the Red Planet. For almost an Earthly year I had been immured within the grim walls of Ras Thavas' bloody laboratory, until, such creatures of habit are we, the weird life there had grown to seem quite natural and ordinary; but with this first glimpse of open country there surged up within me an urge for freedom, for space, for room to move about, such as I knew would not be long denied.

Directly beneath lay an irregular patch of rocky land elevated perhaps a dozen feet or more above the general level of the immediately surrounding country. Its extent was, at a rough guess, a hundred acres. Upon this stood the buildings and grounds, which were enclosed in a high wall. The tower upon which we stood was situated at about the centre of the total area enclosed. Beyond the outer wall was a strip of rocky ground on which grew a sparse forest of fair-sized trees interspersed with patches of a jungle growth, and beyond all, what appeared to be an oozy marsh through which were narrow water courses connecting occasional open water—little lakes, the largest of which could have comprised scarce two acres. This landscape extended as far as the eye could reach, broken by occasional islands similar to that upon which we were, and at a short distance by the skyline of a large city, whose towers and domes and minarets glistened and sparkled in the sun as though plated with shining metals and picked out with precious gems.

This, I knew, must be Toonol and all about us the Great Toonolian Marshes which extend nearly eighteen hundred Earth miles east and west and in some places have a width of three hundred miles. Little is known about them in other portions of Barsoom as they are frequented by fierce beasts, afford no landing places for fliers and are commanded by Phundahl at their western end and Toonol at the east; inhospitable kingdoms that invite no intercourse with the outside world and maintain their independence alone by their inaccessibility and savage aloofness.

As my eyes returned to the island at our feet I saw a huge form emerge from one of the nearby patches of jungle a short distance beyond the outer wall. It was followed by a second and a third. Ras Thavas saw that the creatures had attracted my notice.

'There,' he said, pointing to them, 'are three of a number of similar reasons why it would not have been safe for us to venture outside the enclosure.'

They were great white apes of Barsoom, creatures so savage that even that fierce Barsoomian lion, the banth, hesitates to cross their path.

'They serve two purposes,' explained Ras Thavas. 'They discourage those who might otherwise creep upon me by night from the city of Toonol, where I am not without many good enemies, and they prevent desertion upon the part of my slaves and assistants.'

'But how do your clients reach you?' I asked. 'How are your supplies brought in?'

He turned and pointed down towards the highest portion of the irregular roof of the building below us. Built upon it was a large, shed-like structure. 'There,' he said, 'I keep three small ships. One of them goes every day to Toonol.'

I was overcome with eagerness to know more about these ships, in which I thought I saw a much-needed means of escape from the island; but I dared not question him for fear of arousing his suspicions.

As we turned to descend the tower runway I expressed

interest in the structure, which gave evidence of being far older than any of the surrounding buildings.

'This tower,' said Ras Thavas, 'was built some twenty-three thousand years ago by an ancestor of mine who was driven from Toonol by the reigning jeddak of the time. Here and upon other islands, he gathered a considerable following, dominated the surrounding marshes and defended himself successfully for hundreds of years. While my family has been permitted to return to Toonol since, this has been their home; to which, one by one, have been added the various buildings which you see about the tower, each floor of which connects with the adjacent building from the roof to the lowest pits beneath the ground.'

This information also interested me greatly since I thought that I saw where it too might have considerable bearing upon my plan of escape, and so, as we descended the runway, I encouraged Ras Thavas to discourse upon the construction of the tower, its relation to the other buildings and especially its accessibility from the pits. We walked again in the outer garden and by the time we returned to Ras Thavas' quarters it was almost dark and the master surgeon was considerably fatigued.

'I feel that I shall sleep well tonight,' he said as I left him.

'I hope so, Ras Thavas,' I replied.

ESCAPE

It was usually about three hours after the evening meal, which was served immediately after dark, that the establishment quieted down definitely for the night. While I should have preferred waiting longer before undertaking that which I had in mind, I could not safely do so, since there was much to be accomplished before dawn. So it was that with the first indications that the occupants of the building in which my work was to be performed had retired for the night, I left my quarters and went directly to the laboratory, where, fortunately for my plans, the bodies of Gor Hajus, the assassin of Toonol, and 378-J-493811-P both reposed. It was the work of a few minutes to carry them to adjoining tables, where I quickly strapped them securely against the possibility that one or both of them might not be willing to agree to the proposition I was about to make them, and thus force me to anaesthetize them again. At last the incisions were made, the tubes attached and the motors started. 378-J-493811-P, whom I shall hereafter call by his own name Dar Tarus, was the first to open his eyes; but he had not regained full consciousness when Gor Hajus showed signs of life.

I waited until both appeared quite restored. Dar Tarus was eyeing me with growing recognition that brought a most venomous expression of hatred to his countenance. Gor Hajus was frankly puzzled. The last he remembered was the scene in the death chamber at the instant that his executioner had run a sword through his heart. It was I who broke the silence.

'In the first place,' I said, 'let me tell you where you are, if you do not already know.'

'I know well enough where I am,' growled Dar Tarus.

'Ah!' exclaimed Gor Hajus, whose eyes had been roaming about the chamber. 'I can guess where I am. What Toonolian has not heard of Ras Thavas? So they sold my corpse to the old butcher, did they? And what now? Did I just arrive?'

'You have been here six years,' I told him, 'and you may stay here for ever unless we three can reach an agreement within the next few minutes, and that goes for you too, Dar Tarus.'

'Six years!' mused Gor Hajus. 'Well, out with it, man. What do you want? If it is to slay Ras Thavas, no! He has saved me from utter destruction; but name me some other, preferably Vobis Kan, Jeddak of Toonol. Find me a blade and I will slay a hundred to regain life.'

'I seek the life of none unless he stands in the way of the fulfilment of my desire in this matter that I have in hand. Listen! Ras Thavas had here a beautiful Duhorian girl. He sold her body to Xaxa, Jeddara of Phundahl, transplanting the girl's brain to the wrinkled and hideous body of the jeddara. It is my intention to regain the body, restore it to its own brain and return the girl to Duhor.'

Gor Hajus grinned. 'You have a large contract on your hands,' he said, 'but I can see that you are a man after my own heart and I am with you. It will give freedom and fighting, and all that I ask is a chance for one thrust at Vobis Kan.'

'I promise your life,' I replied; 'but with the understanding that you serve me faithfully and none other, undertaking no business of your own, until mine has been carried to a successful conclusion.'

'That means that I shall have to serve you for life,' he replied, 'for the thing you have undertaken you can never accomplish; but that is better than lying here on a cold ersite slab waiting for old Ras Thavas to come along and carve out my gizzard. I am yours! Let me up, that I may feel a good pair of legs under me again.'

'And you?' I asked, turning to Dar Tarus as I released the bonds that held Gor Hajus. For the first time I now noticed that the ugly expression that I had first noted upon the face of Dar Tarus had given place to one of eagerness.

'Strike off my bonds!' he cried. 'I will follow you to the ends of Barsoom and the way leads thus far to the fulfilment of your design but it will not. It will lead to Phundahl and to the chamber of the wicked Xaxa, where, by the generosity of my ancestors, I may be given the opportunity to avenge the hideous wrong the creature did me. You could not have chosen one better fitted for your mission than Dar Tarus, one time soldier of the Jeddara's Guard, whom she had slain that in my former body one of her rotten nobles might woo the girl I loved.'

A moment later the two men stood at my side, and without more delay I led them towards the runway that descended to the pits beneath the building. As we went, I described to them the creature I had chosen to be the fourth member of our strange party. Gor Hajus questioned the wisdom of my choice, saying that the ape would attract too much attention to us. Dar Tarus, however, believed that it might be helpful in many respects, since it was possible that we might be compelled to spend some time among the islands of the marshes which were often infested with these creatures; while, once in Phundahl, the ape might readily be used in the furtherance of our plans and would cause no considerable comment in a city where many of these beasts are held in captivity and often are seen performing for the edification of street crowds.

We went at once to the vault where the ape lay and where I had concealed the anaesthetized body of Valla Dia. Here I revived the great anthropoid and to my great relief found that the human half of its brain still was dominant. Briefly I explained my plan as I had to the other two and won the hearty promise of his support upon my engaging to restore his brain to its rightful place upon the completion of our venture.

First we must get off the island, and I outlined two plans I had in mind. One was to steal one of Ras Thavas' three fliers and set out directly for Phundahl, and the other, in the event that the first did not seem feasible, was to secrete ourselves aboard one of them on the chance that we might either overpower the crew and take over the ship after we had left the island, or escape undetected upon its arrival in Toonol. Dar Tarus liked the first plan; the ape, whom we now called by the name belonging to the human half of his brain, Hovan Du, preferred the first alternative of the second plan and Gor Hajus the second alternative.

Dar Tarus explained that as our principal objective was Phundahl, the quicker we got there the better. Hovan Du argued that by seizing the ship after it had left the island we would have longer time in which to make our escape before the ship was missed and pursuit instituted, than by seizing it now in the full knowledge that its absence would be discovered within a few hours. Gor Hajus thought that it would be better if we could come into Toonol secretly and there, through one of his friends, secure arms and a flier of our own. It would never do, he insisted, to attempt to go far without arms for himself and Dar Tarus, nor could we hope to reach Phundahl without being overhauled by pursuers; for we must plan on the hypothesis that Ras Thavas would immediately discover my absence; that he would go at once to investigate; that he would find Dar Tarus and Gor Hajus missing and thereupon lose no time in advising Vobis Kan, Jeddak of Toonol, that Gor Hajus the assassin was at large, whereupon the Jeddak's best ships would be sent in pursuit.

Gor Hajus's reasoning was sound, and coupled with my recollection that Ras Thavas had told me that his three ships were slow, I could readily foresee that our liberty would be of short duration were we to steal one of the old surgeon's fliers.

As we discussed the matter we had made our way through the pits and I had found the exit to the tower. Silently we passed upward along the runway and out upon the roof. Both moons were winging low through the heavens and the scene was almost as light as day. If anyone was about discovery was certain. We hastened towards the hangar and were soon within it, where, for a moment at least, I breathed far more easily than I had beneath those two brilliant moons upon the exposed roof.

The fliers were peculiar looking contrivances, low, squat, with rounded bows and sterns and covered decks, their every line proclaiming them as cargo carriers built for anything but speed. One was much smaller than the other two and a second was evidently undergoing repairs. The third I entered and examined carefully. Gor Hajus was with me and pointed out several places where we might hide with little likelihood of discovery unless it were suspected that we might be aboard, and that of course constituted a very real danger; so much so that I had about decided to risk all aboard the small flier, which Gor Hajus assured me would be the fastest of the three, when Dar Tarus stuck his head into the ship and motioned me to come quickly.

'There is someone about,' he said when I reached his side.

'Where?' I demanded.

'Come,' he said, and led me to the rear of the hangar, which was flush with the wall of the building upon which it stood, and pointed through one of the windows into the inner garden where, to my consternation, I saw Ras Thavas walking slowly to and fro. For an instant I was sick with despair, for I knew that no ship could leave that roof unseen while anyone was abroad in the garden beneath, and Ras Thavas least of all people in the world; but suddenly a great light dawned upon me. I called the three close to me and explained my plan.

Instantly they grasped the possibilities in it and a moment later we had run the small flier out upon the roof and turned her nose towards the east, away from Toonol. Then Gor Hajus entered her, set the various controls as we had decided, opened the throttle, slipped back to the roof. The four of us hastened into the hangar and ran to the rear window where we saw the ship moving slowly and gracefully out over the garden and the head of Ras Thavas, whose ears must instantly have caught the faint purring of the motor, for he was looking up by the time we reached the window.

Instantly he hailed the ship and stepping back from the window that he might not see me I answered: 'Good-bye, Ras Thavas! It is I, Vad Varo, going out into a strange world to see what it is like. I shall return. The spirits of your ancestors be with you until then.' That was a phrase I had picked up from reading in Ras Thavas' library and I was quite proud of it.

'Come back at once,' he shouted up in reply, 'or you will be with the spirits of your own ancestors before another day is done.'

I made no reply. The ship was now at such a distance that I feared my voice might no longer seem to come from it and that we should be discovered. Without more delay we concealed ourselves aboard one of the remaining fliers, that upon which no work was being done, and there commenced as long and tiresome a period of waiting as I can recall ever having passed through.

I had at last given up any hope of the ship's being flown that day when I heard voices in the hangar, and presently the sound of footsteps aboard the flier. A moment later a few commands were given and almost immediately the ship moved slowly out into the open.

The four of us were crowded into a small compartment built into a tiny space between the forward and aft starboard buoyancy tanks. It was very dark and poorly ventilated, having evidently been designed as a storage closet to utilize otherwise waste space. We dared not converse for fear of attracting attention to our presence, and for the same reason we moved about as little as possible, since we had no means of knowing but that some member of the crew might be just beyond the thin door that separated us from the main cabin of the ship. Altogether we were most uncomfortable; but the distance to Toonol is not so great but that we might hope that our situation would soon be changed—at least if Toonol was to be the destination of the ship. Of this we soon had cheering hope. We had been out but a short time when, faintly, we heard a hail and then the motors were immediately shut down and the ship stopped.

'What ship?' we heard a voice demand, and from aboard our own came the reply:

'The Vosar, Tower of Thavas for Toonol.' We heard a scraping as the other ship touched ours.

'We are coming aboard to search you in the name of Vobis Kan, Jeddak of Toonol. Make way!' shouted one from the other ship. Our cheer had been of short duration. We heard the shuffling of many feet and Gor Hajus whispered in my ear.

'What shall we do?' he asked.

I slipped my short-sword into his hand. 'Fight!' I replied.

'Good, Vad Varo,' he replied, and then I handed him my pistol and told him to pass it on to Dar Tarus. We heard the voices again, but nearer now.

'What ho!' cried one. 'It is Bal Zak himself, my old friend Bal Zak!'

'None other,' replied a deep voice. 'And whom did you expect to find in command of the Vosar other than Bal Zak?'

'Who could know but that it might have been this Vad

Varo himself, or even Gor Hajus,' said the other, 'and our orders are to search all ships.'

'I would that they were here,' replied Bal Zak, 'for the reward is high. But how could they, when Ras Thavas himself with his own eyes saw them fly off in the Pinsar before dawn this day and disappear in the east?'

'Right you are, Bal Zak,' agreed the other, 'and it were a waste of time to search your ship. Come, men! to our own!'

I could feel the muscles about my heart relax with the receding footfalls of Vobis Kan's warriors as they quitted the deck of the Vosar for their own ship, and my spirits rose with the renewed purring of our own motor as Ras Thavas' flier again got under way. Gor Hajus bent his lips close to my ear.

'The spirits of our ancestors smile upon us,' he whispered. 'It is night and the darkness will aid in covering our escape from the ship and the landing stage.

'What makes you think it is night?' I asked.

'Vobis Kan's ship was close by when it hailed and asked our name. By daylight it could have seen what ship we were.'

He was right. We had been locked in that stuffy hole since before dawn, and while I had thought that it had been for a considerable time, I also had realized that the darkness and the inaction and the nervous strain would tend to make it seem much longer than it really had been; so that I would not have been greatly surprised had we made Toonol by daylight.

The distance from the Tower of Thavas to Toonol is inconsiderable, so that shortly after Vobis Kan's ship had hailed us we came to rest upon the landing stage at our destination. For a long time we waited, listening to the sounds of movement aboard the ship and wondering, upon my part at least, as to what the intentions of the captain might be. It was quite possible that Bal Zak might return to Thavas this same night, especially if he had come to Toonol to fetch a rich or powerful patient to the laboratories but if he had come only for supplies he might well lie here until the morrow. This much I had learned from Gor Hajus, my own knowledge of the movements of the fliers of Ras Thavas being considerably less than nothing; for, though I had been months a lieutenant of the master surgeon, I had learned only the day before of the existence of his small fleet, it being according to the policy of Ras Thavas to tell me nothing unless the telling of it coincided with and furthered his own plans.

Questions which I asked he always answered, if he reasoned that the effects would not be harmful to his own interests, but he volunteered nothing that he did not particularly wish me to know; and the fact that there were no windows in the outside walls of the buildings facing towards Toonol, that I had never before the previous day been upon the roof and that I never had seen a ship sail over the inner court towards the east all tended to explain my ignorance of the fleet and its customary operations.

We waited quietly until silence fell upon the ship, betokening either that the crew had retired for the night or that they had gone down into the city. Then, after a whispered consultation with Gor Hajus, we decided to make an attempt to leave the flier. It was our purpose to seek a hiding place within the tower of the landing stage from which we might investigate possible avenues of escape into the city, either at once or upon the morrow when we might more easily mix with the crowd that Gor Hajus said would certainly be in evidence from a few hours after sunrise.

Cautiously I opened the door of our closet and looked into the main cabin beyond. It lay in darkness. Silently we filed out. The silence of the tomb lay upon the flier, but from far below arose the subdued noises of the city. So far, so good! Then, without sound, without warning, a burst of brilliant light illuminated the interior of the cabin. I felt my fingers tighten upon my sword hilt as I glanced quickly about.

Directly opposite us, in the narrow doorway of a small cabin, stood a tall man whose handsome harness betokened the fact that he was no common warrior. In either hand he held a heavy Barsoomian pistol, into the muzzles of which we found ourselves staring.

HANDS UP!

In quiet tones he spoke the words of the Barsoomian equivalent of our earthly *hands up!* The shadow of a grim smile touched his lips, and as he saw us hesitate to obey his commands he spoke again.

'Do as I tell you and you will be well off. Keep perfect silence. A raised voice may spell your doom; a pistol shot most assuredly.'

Gor Hajus raised his hands above his head and we others followed his example.

'I am Bal Zak,' announced the stranger. My heart slumped.

'Then you had better commence firing,' said Gor Hajus, 'for you will not take us alive and we are four to one.'

'Not so fast, Gor Hajus,' admonished the captain of the Vosar, 'until you learn what is in my mind.'

'That we already know, for we heard you speak of the large reward that awaited the captor of Vad Varo and Gor Hajus,' snapped the assassin of Toonol.

'Had I craved that reward so much I could have turned you over to the dwar of Vobis Kan's ship when he boarded us,' said Bal Zak.

'You did not know we were aboard the Vosar,' I reminded him.

'Ah, but I did.'

Gor Hajus snorted his disbelief.

'How then,' Bal Zak reminded us, 'was I able to be ready upon this very spot when you emerged from your hiding place? Yes, I knew that you were aboard.'

'But how?' demanded Dar Tarus.

'It is immaterial,' replied Bal Zak, 'but to satisfy your

natural curiosity I will tell you that I have quarters in a small room in the Tower of Thavas, my windows overlook the roof and the hangar. My long life spent aboard fliers has made me very sensitive to every sound of a ship—motors changing their speed will awaken me in the dead of night, as quickly as will their starting or their stopping. I was awakened by the starting of the motors of the Pinsar; I saw three of you upon the roof and the fourth drop from the deck of the flier as she started and my judgement told me that the ship was being sent out unmanned for some reason of which I had no knowledge. It was too late for me to prevent the act and so I waited in silence to learn what would follow. I saw you hasten into the hangar and I heard Ras Thavas' hail and your reply, and then I saw you board the Vosar. Immediately I descended to the roof and ran noiselessly to the hangar, apprehending that you intended making away with this ship; but there was no one about the controls; and from a tiny port in the control room, through which one has a view of the main cabin, I saw you enter that closet. I was at once convinced that your only purpose was to stow away for Toonol and consequently, aside from keeping an eye upon your hiding place, I went about my business as usual.'

'And you did not advise Ras Thavas?' I asked.

'I advised no one,' he replied. 'Years ago I learned to mind my own business, to see all, to hear all and to tell nothing unless it profited me to do so.'

'But you said that the reward is high for our apprehension,' Gor Hajus reminded him. 'Would it not be profitable to collect it?'

'There are in the breasts of honourable men,' replied Bal Zak, 'forces that rise superior to the lust for gold, and while Toonolians are supposedly a people free from the withering influences of sentiment yet I for one am not totally unconscious of the demand of gratitude. Six years ago, Gor Hajus, you refused to assassinate my father, holding that he was a good man, worthy to live and one that had once befriended you slightly. Today, through his son, you reap your reward and in some measure are repaid for the punishment that was meted out to you by Vobis Kan because of your refusal to slay the sire of Bal Zak. I have sent my crew away that none aboard the Vosar but myself might have knowledge of your presence. Tell me your plans and command me in what way I may be of further service to you.'

'We wish to reach the streets, unobserved,' replied Gor Hajus. 'Can you but help us in that we shall not put upon your shoulders further responsibility for our escape. You have our gratitude and in Toonol, I need not remind you, the gratitude of Gor Hajus is a possession that even the Jeddak has craved.'

'Your problem is complicated,' said Bal Zak, after a moment of thought, 'by the personnel of your party. The ape would immediately attract attention and arouse suspicion. Knowing much of Ras Thavas' experiments I realized at once this morning, after watching him with you, that he had the brain of a man; but this very fact would attract to him and to you the closer attention of the masses.'

'I do not need acquaint them with the fact,' growled Hovan Du. 'To them I need be but a captive ape. Are such unknown in Toonol?'

'Not entirely, though they are rare,' replied Bal Zak. 'But there is also the white skin of Vad Varo! Ras Thavas appears to have known nothing of the presence of the ape with you; but he full well knew of Vad Varo, and your description has been spread by every means at his command. You would be recognized immediately by the first Toonolian that lays eyes upon you, and then there is Gor Hajus. He has been as dead for six years, yet I venture there is scarce a Toonolian that broke the shell prior to ten years ago who does not know the face of Gor Hajus as well as he knows that of his own mother. The Jeddak himself was not better known to the people of Toonol than Gor Hajus. That leaves but one who might possibly escape suspicion and detection in the streets of Toonol.'

'If we could but obtain weapons for these others,' I suggested, 'we might even yet reach the house of Gor Hajus' friend.'

'Fight your way through the city of Toonol?' demanded Bal Zak.

'If there is no other way we should have to,' I replied.

'I admire the will,' commented the commander of the Vosar, 'but fear that the flesh is without sufficient strength Wait! there is a way—perhaps. On the stage just below this there is a public depot where equilibrimotors are kept and rented. Could we find the means to obtain four of these there would be a chance, at least, for you to elude the air patrols and reach the house of Gor Hajus' friend; and I think I see a way to the accomplishment of that. The landing tower is closed for the night but there are several watchmen distributed through it at different levels. There is one at the equilibrimotor depot and, as I happen to know, he is a devotee of jetan. He would rather play jetan than attend to his duties as watchman. I often remain aboard the Vosar at night and occasionally he and I indulge in a game. I will ask him up tonight and while he is thus engaged you may go to the depot, help yourselves to equilibrimotors and pray to your ancestors that no air patrol suspicions you as you cross the city towards your destination. What think you of this plan, Gor Hajus?'

'It is splendid,' replied the assassin. 'And you, Vad Varo?'

'If I knew what an equilibrimotor is I might be in a better position to judge the merits of the plan,' I replied. 'However, I am satisfied to abide by the judgement of Gor Hajus. I can assure you, Bal Zak of our great appreciation, and as Gor Hajus has put the stamp of his approval upon your plan I can only urge you to arrange that we may put it into effect with as little delay as possible.'

'Good!' exclaimed Bal Zak. 'Come with me and I will conceal you until I have lured the watchman to the jetan game within my cabin. After that your fate will be in your own hands.'

We followed him from the ship on to the deck of the landing stage and close under the side of the Vosar opposite that from which the watchman must approach the ship and enter it. Then, bidding us good luck, Bal Zak departed.

From the summit of the landing tower I had my first view of a Martian city. Several hundred feet below me lay spread the broad, well lighted avenues of Toonol, many of which were crowded with people. Here and there, in this central district, a building was raised high upon its supporting, cylindrical metal shaft while further out, where the residences predominated, the city took on the appearance of a colossal and grotesque forest. Among the larger palaces only an occasional suite of rooms was thus raised high above the level of the others, these being the sleeping apartments of the owners, their servants or their guests; but the smaller homes were raised in their entirety, a precaution necessitated by the constant activities of the followers of Gor Hajus' ancient profession that permitted no man to be free from the constant menace of assassination. Throughout the central district the sky was pierced by the lofty towers of several other landing stages but, as I was later to learn, these were comparatively few in number. Toonol is in no sense a flying nation, supporting no such enormous fleets of merchant ships and vessels of war as, for example, the twin cities of Helium or the great capital of Ptarth.

A peculiar feature of the street lighting of Toonol, and in fact the same condition applies to the lighting of other Barsoomian cities I have visited, I noted for the first time that night as I waited upon the landing stage for the return of Bal Zak with the watchman. The luminosity below me seemed confined directly to the area to be lighted; there was no diffusion of light upwards or beyond the limits the lamps were designed to light. This was effected, I was told, by lamps designed upon principles resulting from ages of investigation of the properties of light waves and the laws governing them which permit Barsoomian scientists to confine and control light as we confine and control matter. The light waves leave the lamp, pass along a prescribed circuit and return to the lamp. There is no waste nor, strange this seemed to me, are there any dense shadows when lights are properly installed and adjusted; for the waves, in passing around objects to return to the lamp, illuminate all sides of them.

The effect of this lighting from the great height of the tower was rather remarkable. The night was dark, there being no moons at that hour upon this night, and the effect was that obtained when sitting in a darkened auditorium and looking upon a brilliantly lighted stage. I was still intent upon watching the life and colour beneath when we heard Bal Zak returning. That he had been successful in his mission was apparent from the fact that he was conversing with another.

Five minutes later we crept quietly from our hiding place and descended to the stage below where lay the equilibrimotor depot. As theft is practically unknown upon Barsoom, except for purposes entirely disassociated from a desire to obtain pecuniary profit through the thing stolen, no precautions are taken against theft. We therefore found the doors of the depot open and Gor Hajus and Dar Tarus quickly selected four equilibrimotors and adjusted them upon us. They consist of a broad belt, not unlike the life-belt used aboard transoceanic liners upon Earth; these belts are filled with the eighth Barsoomian ray, or ray of propulsion, to a sufficient degree to just about equalize the pull of gravity and thus to maintain a person in equilibrium between that force and the opposite force exerted by the eighth ray. Permanently attached to the back of the belt is a small radium motor, the controls for which are upon the front of the belt. Rigidly attached to and projecting from each side of the upper rim of the belt is a strong, light wing with small hand levers for quickly altering its position.

Gor Hajus quickly explained the method of control, but I could apprehend that there might be embarrassment and trouble awaiting me before I mastered the art of flying in an equilibrimotor. He showed me how to tilt the wings downwards in walking so that I would not leave the ground at every step, and thus he led me to the edge of the landing stage.

'We will rise here,' he said, 'and keeping in the darkness of the upper levels seek to reach the house of my friend without being detected. If we are pursued by air patrol we must separate and later those who escape may gather just west of the city wall where you will find a small lake with a deserted tower upon its northern rim—this tower will be our rendezvous in event of trouble. Follow me!' He started his motor and rose gracefully into the air.

Hovan Du followed him and then it was my turn. I rose beautifully for about twenty feet, floating out over the city which lay hundreds of feet below, and then, quite suddenly, I turned upside-down. I had done something wrong—I was quite positive of it. It was a most startling sensation, I can assure you, floating there with my head down, quite helpless; while below me lay the streets of a great city and no softer, I was sure, than the streets of Los Angeles or Paris. My motor was still going and as I manipulated the controls which operated the wings I commenced to describe all sorts of strange loops and spirals and spins and then Dar Tarus came to my rescue. First he told me to lie quietly and then directed the manipulation of each wing until I had gained an upright position. After that I did fairly well and was soon rising in the wake of Gor Hajus and Hovan Du.

I need not describe in detail the hour of flying, or rather

floating, that ensued. Gor Hajus led us to a considerable altitude and there, through the darkness above the city, our slow motors drove us towards a district of magnificent homes surrounded by spacious grounds and here, as we hovered over a large palace, we were suddenly startled by a sharp challenge coming from directly above us.

'Who flies by night?' a voice demanded.

'Friends of Mu Tel, Prince of the House of Kan,' replied Gor Hajus quickly.

'Let me see your night flying permit and your flier's licence,' ordered the one above us, at the same time swooping suddenly to our level and giving me my first sight of a Martian policeman. He was equipped with a much swifter and handier equilibrimotor than ours. I think that was the first fact to impress us deeply, and it demonstrated the futility of flight; for he could have given us ten minutes' start and overhauled each of us within another ten minutes, even though we had elected to fly in different directions. The fellow was a warrior rather than a policeman, though detailed to duty such as our earthly police officers perform; the city being patrolled both day and night by the warriors of Vobis Kan's army.

He dropped now close to the assassin of Toonol, again demanding permit and licence and at the same time flashing a light in the face of my comrade.

'By the sword of the Jeddak!' he cried. 'Fortune heaps her favours upon me. Who would have thought an hour since that it would be I who would collect the reward for the capture of Gor Hajus?'

'Any other fool might have thought it,' returned Gor Hajus, 'but he would have been as wrong as you,' and as he spoke he struck with the short-sword I had loaned him.

The blow was broken by the wing of the warrior's equilibrimotor, which it demolished, yet it inflicted a severe wound in the fellow's shoulder. He tried to back off, but the damaged wing caused him only to wheel around erratically; and then he seized upon his whistle and attempted to blow a mighty blast that was cut short by another blow from Gor Hajus' sword that split the man's head open to the bridge of his nose.

'Quick!' cried the assassin. 'We must drop into the gardens of Mu Tel, for that signal will bring a swarm of air patrols about our heads.'

The others I saw falling rapidly towards the ground, but again I had trouble. Depress my wings as I would I moved only slightly downward and upon a path that, if continued, would have landed me at a considerable distance from the gardens of Mu Tel. I was approaching one of the elevated portions of the palace, what appeared to be a small suite that was raised upon its shining metal shaft far above the ground. From all directions I could hear the screaming whistles of the air patrols answering the last call of their comrade whose corpse floated just above me, a guide even in death to point the way for his fellows to search us out. They were sure to discover him and then I would be in plain view of them and my fate sealed.

Perhaps I could find ingress to the apartments looming darkly near! There I might hide until the danger had passed, provided I could enter, undetected. I directed my course towards the structure; an open window took form through the darkness and then I collided with a fine wire netting—I had run into a protecting curtain that fends off assassins of the air from these high-flung sleeping apartments. I felt that I was lost. If I could but reach the ground I might find concealment among the trees and shrubbery that I had seen vaguely outlined beneath me in the gardens of this Barsoomian prince; but I could not drop at a sufficient angle to bring me to ground within the garden, and when I tried to spiral down I turned over and started up again. I thought of ripping open my belt and letting the eighth ray escape; but in my unfamiliarity with this strange force I feared that such an act might precipitate me to the ground with too great violence, though I was determined to have recourse to it as a last alternative if nothing less drastic presented itself.

In my last attempt to spiral downward I rose rapidly feet foremost to a sudden and surprising collision with some object above me. As I frantically righted myself, fully expecting to be immediately seized by a member of the air patrol, I found myself face to face with the corpse of the warrior Gor Hajus had slain. The whistling of the air patrols sounded ever nearer—it could be only a question of seconds now before I was discovered—and with the stern necessity that confronted me, with death looking me in the face, there burst upon me a possible avenue of escape from my dilemma.

Seizing tightly with my left hand the harness of the dead Toonolian, I whipped out my dagger and slashed his buoyancy belt a dozen times. Instantly, as the rays escaped, his body started to drag me downward. Our descent was rapid, but not precipitate, and it was but a matter of seconds before we landed gently upon the scarlet sward of the gardens of Mu Tel, Prince of the House of Kan, close beside a clump of heavy shrubbery. Above me sounded the whistles of the circling patrols as I dragged the corpse of the warrior into the concealing depth of the foliage. Nor was I an instant too soon for safety, as almost immediately the brilliant rays of a searchlight shot downward from the deck of a small patrol ship, illuminating the open spaces of the garden all about me. A hurried glance through the branches and the leaves of my sanctuary revealed nothing of my companions and I breathed a sigh of relief in the thought that they, too, had found concealment.

The light played for a short time about the gardens and then passed on, as did the sound of the patrol's whistles, as the search proceeded elsewhere thus giving me the assurance that no suspicion was directed upon our hiding place.

Left in darkness I appropriated such of the weapons of the dead warrior as I coveted, after having removed my equilibrimotor, which I was first minded to destroy, but which I finally decided to moor to one of the larger shrubs against the possibility that I might again have need for it; and now, secure in the conviction that the danger of discovery by the air patrol had passed, I left my concealment and started in search of my companions.

Keeping well in the shadows of the trees and shrubs I moved in the direction of the main building, which loomed darkly near at hand; for in this direction I believed Gor Hajus would lead the others as I knew that the palace of Mu Tel was to have been our destination. As I crept along, moving with utmost stealth, Thuria, the nearer moon, shot suddenly above the horizon, illuminating the night with her brilliant rays. I was close to the building's ornately carved wall at the moment, beside me was a narrow niche, its interior cast in deepest shadow by Thuria's brilliant rays; to my left was an open bit of lawn upon which, revealed in every detail of its terrifying presence, stood as fearsome a creature as my earthly eyes ever had rested upon. It was a beast about the size of a Shetland pony, with ten short legs and a terrifying head that bore some slight resemblance to that of a frog, except that the jaws were equipped with three rows of long, sharp tusks.

The thing had its nose in the air and was sniffing about, while its great pop eyes moved swiftly here and there, assuring me, beyond the shadow of a doubt, that it was searching for someone. I am not inclined to be egotistical, yet I could not avoid the conviction that it was searching for me. It was my first experience of a Martian watch-dog; and as I sought concealment within the dark shadows of the niche behind me, at the very instant that the creature's eyes alighted upon me, and heard his growl and saw him charge straight towards me, I had a premonition that it might prove my last experience with one.

I drew my long-sword as I backed into the niche, but with a sense of utter inadequacy of the unaccustomed weapon in the face of this three or four hundred pounds of ferocity incarnate. Slowly I backed away into the shadows as the creature bore down upon me and then, as it entered the niche, my back collided with a solid obstacle that put an end to further retreat.

THE PALACE OF MU TEL

As the calot entered the niche I experienced, I believe, all of the reactions of the cornered rat, and I certainly know that I set myself to fight in that proverbial manner. The beast was almost upon me and I was metaphorically kicking myself for not having remained in the open where there were many tall trees when the support at my back suddenly gave way, a hand reached out of the darkness behind me and seized my harness and I was drawn swiftly into inky blackness. A door slammed and the silhouette of the calot against the moonlit entrance to the niche was blotted out.

A gruff voice spoke in my ear. 'Come with me!' it said. A hand found mine and thus I was led along through the darkness of what I soon discovered was a narrow corridor from the constantly recurring collisions I had first with one side of it and then with the other.

Ascending gradually, the corridor turned abruptly at right angles and I saw beyond my guide a dim luminosity that gradually increased until another turn brought us to the threshold of a brilliantly lighted chamber—a magnificent apartment, the gorgeous furnishings and decorations of which beggar the meagre descriptive powers of my native tongue. Gold, ivory, precious stones, marvellous woods, resplendent fabrics, gorgeous furs and startling architecture combined to impress upon my earthly vision such a picture as I had never even dreamed of dreaming; and in the centre of this room, surrounded by a little group of Martians, were my three companions.

My guide conducted me towards the party, the members of which had turned towards us as we entered the chamber, and stopped before a tall Barsoomian, resplendent in jewel encrusted harness.

'Prince,' he said, 'I was scarce a tal too soon. In fact, as I opened the door to step out into the garden in search of him, as you directed, there he was upon the opposite side with one of the calots of the garden almost upon him.'

'Good!' exclaimed he who had been addressed as prince, and then he turned to Gor Hajus. 'This is he, my friend, of whom you told me?'

'This is Vad Varo, who claims to be from the planet Jasoom,' replied Gor Hajus; 'and this, Vad Varo, is Mu Tel, Prince of the House of Kan.'

I bowed and the prince advanced and placed his right hand upon my left shoulder in true Barsoomian acknowledgment of an introduction; when I had done similarly, the ceremony was over. There was no silly pleased-to-meet-you, how-do-you-do? or it's-a-pleasure-I-assure-you.

At Mu Tel's request I narrated briefly what had befallen me between the time I had become separated from my companions and the moment that one of his officers had snatched me from impending disaster. Mu Tel gave instructions that all traces of the dead patrol be removed before dawn lest their discovery bring upon him the further suspicion of his uncle, Vobis Kan, Jeddak of Toonol, whom it seemed had long been jealous of his nephew's growing popularity and fearful that he harboured aspirations for the throne.

It was later in the evening, during one of those elaborate meals for which the princes of Barsoom are justly famous, when mellowed slightly by the rare vintages with which he delighted his guests, that Mu Tel discoursed with less restraint upon his imperial uncle.

'The nobles have long been tired of Vobis Kan,' he said, 'and the people are tiring of him—he is a conscienceless tyrant—but he is our hereditary ruler, and so they hesitate to change. We are a practical people, little influenced by sentiment; yet there is enough to keep the masses loyal to their jeddak even after he has ceased to deserve their loyalty, while the fear of the wrath of the masses keeps the nobles loyal. There is also the natural suspicion that I, the next in line for succession, would make them no less tyrannical a jeddak than has Vobis Kan, while, having youth, I might be much more active in cruel and nefarious practices.

'For myself, I would not hesitate to destroy my uncle and

seize his throne were I sure of the support of the army, for with the warriors of Vobis Kan at my back I might defy the balance of Toonol. It is because of this that I long since offered my friendship to Gor Hajus; not that he might slay my uncle, but that when I had slain him in fair fight Gor Hajus might win to me the loyalty of the jeddak's warriors, for great is the popularity of Gor Hajus among the soldiers, who ever look up to such a great fighter with reverence and devotion. I have offered Gor Hajas a high place in the affairs of Toonol should he cast his lot with me; but he tells me that he has first to fulfil his obligations to you, Vad Varo, and for the furtherance of your adventure he has asked me to give you what assistance I may. This I offer gladly, from purely practical motives, since your early success will hasten mine. Therefore I propose to place at your disposal a staunch flier that will carry you and your companions to Phundahl.'

This offer I naturally accepted, after which we fell to discussing plans for our departure which we finally decided to attempt early the following night, at a time when neither of the moons would be in the heavens. After a brief discussion of equipment we were, at my request, permitted to retire since I had not slept for more than thirty-six hours and my companions for twenty-four.

Slaves conducted us to our sleeping apartments, which were luxuriously furnished, and arranged magnificent sleeping silks and furs for our comfort. After they had left us Gor Hajus touched a button and the room rose swiftly upon its metal shaft to a height of forty or fifty feet; the wire netting automatically dropped about us, and we were safe for the night.

The following morning, after our apartment had been lowered to its daylight level and before I was permitted to leave it, a slave was sent to me by Mu Tel with instructions to stain my entire body the beautiful copper-red of my Barsoomian friends; furnishing me with a disguise which I well knew to be highly essential to the success of my venture, since my white skin would have drawn unpleasant notice upon me in any city of Barsoom. Another slave brought harness and weapons for Gor Hajus, Dar Tarus and myself, and a collar and chain for Hovan Du, the ape-man. Our harness, while of heavy material and splendid workmanship, was quite plain, being free of all insignia either of rank or service—such harness as is customarily worn by the Barsoomian panthan, or soldier of fortune, at such times as he is not definitely in the service of any nation or individual. These panthans are virtually men without a country, being roving mercenaries ready to sell their swords to the highest bidder. Although they have no organization they are ruled by a severe code of ethics and while in the employ of a master are, almost without exception, loyal to him. They are generally supposed to be men who have flown from the wrath of their own jeddaks or the justice of their own courts, but there is among them a sprinkling of adventurous souls who have adopted their calling because of the thrills and excitement it offers. While they are well paid, they are also great gamblers and notorious spenders, with the result that they are almost always without funds and often reduced to strange expedients for the gaining of their livelihoods between engagements; a fact which gave great plausibility to our possession of a trained ape, which upon Mars would appear no more remarkable than would to us the possession of a monkey or parrot by an old salt just returned, from a long cruise, to one of our Earthly ports.

This day that I stayed in the palace of Mu Tel I spent much in the company of the prince, who found pleasure in questioning me concerning the customs, the politics, the civilization and the geography of Earth, with much of which, I was surprised to note, he seemed quite familiar; a fact which he explained was due to the marvellous development of Barsoomian astronomical instruments, wireless photography and wireless telephony; the last of which has been brought to such a state of perfection that many Barsoomian savants have succeeded in learning several Earthly languages, notably Urdu, English and Russian, and, a few, Chinese also. These have doubtless been the first languages to attract their attention because of the fact that they are spoken by great numbers of people over large areas of the world.

Mu Tel took me to a small auditorium in his palace that reminded me somewhat of private projection rooms on Earth. It had, I should say, a capacity of some two hundred persons and was built like a large camera obscura; the audience sitting within the instrument, their backs towards the lens and in front of them, filling one entire end of the room, a large ground glass upon which is thrown the image to be observed.

Mu Tel seated himself at a table upon which was a chart of the heavens. Just above the chart was a movable arm carrying a pointer. This pointer Mu Tel moved until it rested upon the planet Earth, then he switched off the light in the room and immediately there appeared upon the ground glass plate a view such as one might obtain from an aeroplane riding at an elevation of a thousand feet. There was something strangely familiar about the scene before me. It was of a desolate, wasted country. I saw shattered stumps whose orderly arrangement proclaimed that here once an orchard had blossomed and borne fruit. There were great, unsightly holes in the earth and over and across all a tangle of barbed wire. I asked Mu Tel how we might change the picture to another locality. He lighted a small radio bulb between us and I saw a globe there, a globe of Earth, and a small pointer fixed over it.

'The side of this globe now presented to you represents the face of the Earth turned towards us,' explained Mu Tel. 'You will note that the globe is slowly revolving. Place this pointer where you will upon the globe and that portion of Jasoom will be revealed for you.'

I moved the pointer very slowly and the picture changed. A ruined village came into view. I saw some people moving among its ruins. They were not soldiers. A little further on I came upon trenches and dug-outs—there were no soldiers here, either. I moved the pointer rapidly north and south along a vast line of trenches. Here and there in villages there were soldiers, but they were all French soldiers and never were they in the trenches. There were no German soldiers and no fighting. The war was over, then! I moved the pointer to the Rhine and across. There were soldiers in Germany—French soldiers, English soldiers, American soldiers. We had won the war! I was glad, but it seemed very far away and quite unreal—as though no such world existed and no such peoples had ever fought—it was as though I were recalling through its illustrations a novel that I had read a long time since.

'You seem much interested in that war-torn country,' remarked Mu Tel.

'Yes,' I explained, 'I fought in that war. Perhaps I was killed. I do not know.'

'And you won?' he asked.

'Yes, my people won,' I replied. 'We fought for a great principle and for the peace and happiness of a world. I hope that we did not fight in vain.'

'If you mean that you hope that your principle will triumph because you fought and won, or that peace will come, your hopes are futile. War never brought peace—it but brings more and greater wars. War is Nature's natural state—it is folly to combat it. Peace should be considered only as a time for preparation for the principal business of man's existence. Were it not for constant warring of one form of life upon another, and even upon itself, the planets would be so over-run with life that it would smother itself out. We found upon Barsoom that long periods of peace brought plagues and terrible diseases that killed more than the wars killed and in a much more hideous and painful way. There is neither pleasure nor thrill nor reward of any sort to be gained by dying in bed of a loathesome disease. We must all die—let us therefore go out and die in a great and exciting game, and make room for the millions who are to follow us. We have tried it out upon Barsoom and we would not be without war.'

Mu Tel told me much that day about the peculiar philosophy of Toonolians. They believe that no good deed was ever performed except for a selfish motive; they have no god and no religion; they believe, as do all educated Barsoomians, that man came originally from the Tree of Life, but unlike most of their fellows they do not believe that an omnipotent being created the Tree of Life. They hold that the only sin is failure—success, however achieved, is meritorious; and yet, paradoxical as it may seem, they never break their given word. Mu Tel explained that they overcame the baneful results of this degrading weakness—this sentimental bosh—by seldom, if ever, binding themselves to loyalty to another, and then only for a definitely prescribed period.

As I came to know them better, and especially Gor Hajus, I began to realize that much of their flaunted contempt of the finer sensibilities was specious. It is true that generations of inhibition had to some extent atrophied those characteristics of heart and soul which the noblest among us so highly esteem; that friendship's ties were lax and that blood kinship awakened no high sense of responsibility or love even between parents and children; yet Gor Hajus was essentially a man of sentiment, though he would doubtless have run through the heart any who had dared accuse him of it, thus perfectly proving the truth of the other's accusation. His pride in his reputation for integrity and loyalty proved him a man of heart as truly as did his jealousy of his reputation for heartlessness prove him a man of sentiment; and in all this he was but typical of the people of Toonol. They denied deity, and in the same breath worshipped the fetish of science that they had permitted to obsess them quite as harmfully as do religious fanatics accept the unreasoning rule of their imaginary gods; and so, with all their vaunted knowledge, they were unintelligent because unbalanced.

As the day drew to a close I became the more anxious to be away. Far to the west across desolate leagues of marsh lay Phundahl, and in Phundahl the beauteous body of the girl I loved and that I was sworn to restore to its rightful owner. The evening meal was over and Mu Tel himself had conducted us to a secret hangar in one of the towers of his palace. Here artisans had prepared a flier for us, having removed during the day all signs of its real ownership, even to slightly altering its lines; so that in the event of capture Mu Tel's name might in no way be connected with the expedition. Provisions were stored, including plenty of raw meat for Hovan Du, and, as the farther moon sank below the horizon and darkness fell, a panel of the tower wall, directly in front of the flier's nose, slid aside. Mu Tel wished us luck and the ship slipped silently out into the night. The flier, like many of her type, was without cockpit or cabin; a low, metal handrail surmounted her gunwale; heavy rings were set substantially in her deck and to these her crew was supposed to cling or attach themselves by means of their harness hooks provided for this and similar purposes; a low wind shield, with a rakish slant, afforded some protection from the wind; the motor and controls were all exposed, as all the space below decks was taken up by the buoyancy tanks. In this type everything is sacrificed to speed; there is no comfort aboard. When moving at high speed each member of the crew lies extended at full length upon the deck, each in his allotted place to give the necessary trim, and hangs on for dear life. These Toonolian craft, however, are not over fast, so I was told, being far outstripped in speed by the fliers of such nations as Helium and Ptarth, who have for ages devoted themselves to the perfection of their navies; but this one was quite fast enough for our purposes, to the consummation of which it would be pitted against fliers of no higher rating, and it was certainly fast enough for me. In comparison with the slow moving Vosar, it seemed to shoot through the air like an arrow.

We wasted no time in strategy or stealth, but opened her wide as soon as we were in the clear, and directed her straight towards the west and Phundahl. Scarcely had we passed over the gardens of Mu Tel when we met with our first adventure. We shot by a solitary figure floating in the air and almost simultaneously there shrilled forth the warning whistle of an air patrol. A shot whistled above us harmlessly and we were gone; but within a few seconds I saw the rays of a searchlight shining down from above and moving searchingly to and fro through the air.

'A patrol boat!' shouted Gor Hajus in my ear. Hovan Du growled savagely and shook the chain upon his collar. We raced on, trusting to the big gods and the little gods and all our ancestors that that relentless eye of light would not find us out; but it did. Within a few seconds it fell full upon our deck from above and in front of us and there it clung as the patrol boat dropped rapidly towards us while it maintained a high rate of speed upon a course otherwise identical with ours. Then, to our consternation, the ship opened fire on us with explosive bullets. These projectiles contain a high explosive that is detonated by light rays when the opaque covering of the projectile is broken by impact with the target. It is therefore not at all necessary to make a direct hit for a shot to be effective. If the projectile strikes the ground or the deck of a vessel or any solid substance near its target, it does considerably more damage when fired at a group of men than as though it struck but one of them, since it will then explode if its outer shell is broken and kill or wound several; while if it enters the body of an individual the light rays cannot reach it and it accomplishes no more than a non-explosive bullet. Moonlight is not powerful enough to detonate this explosive and so projectiles fired at night, unless touched by the powerful rays of searchlights, detonate at sunrise the following morning, making a battlefield a most unsafe place at that time even though the contending forces are no longer there. Similarly they make the removal of unexploded projectiles from the bodies of the wounded a most ticklish operation which may well result in the instant death of both the patient and the surgeon.

Dar Tarus, at the controls, turned the nose of our flier upwards directly towards the patrol boat and at the same time shouted to us to concentrate our fire upon her propellers. For myself, I could see little but the blinding eye of the searchlight, and at that I fired with the strange weapon to which I had received my first introduction but a few hours since when it was presented to me by Mu Tel. To me that all-searching eye represented the greatest menace that confronted us, and could we blind it the patrol boat would have no great advantage over us. So I kept my rifle straight upon it, my finger on the button that controlled the fire, and prayed for a hit. Gor Hajus knelt at my side, his weapon spitting bullets at the patrol boat. Dar Tarus' hands were busy with the controls and Hovan Du squatted in the bow and growled.

Suddenly Dar Tarus voiced an exclamation of alarm. 'The controls are hit!' he shouted. 'We can't alter our course—the ship is useless.' Almost the same instant the searchlight was extinguished—one of my bullets evidently having found it. We were quite close to the enemy now and heard their shout of anger. Our own craft, out of control, was running swiftly towards the other. It seemed that if there was not a collision we would pass directly beneath the keel of the air patrol. I asked Dar Tarus if our ship was beyond repair.

'We could repair it if we had time,' he replied, 'but it would take hours and while we were thus delayed the whole air patrol force of Toonol would be upon us.'

'Then we must have another ship,' I said.

Dar Tarus laughed. 'You are right, Vad Varo,' he replied, 'but where shall we find it?'

I pointed to the patrol boat. 'We shall not have to look far.'

Dar Tarus shrugged his shoulders. 'Why not!' he exclaimed. 'It would be a glorious fight and a worthy death.'

Gor Hajus slapped me on the shoulder. 'To the death, my captain!' he cried.

Hovan Du shook his chain and roared.

The two ships were rapidly approaching one another. We had stopped firing now for fear that we might disable the craft we hoped to use for our escape; and for some reason the crew of the patrol ship had ceased firing at us—I never learned why. We were moving in a line that would bring us directly beneath the other ship. I determined to board her at all costs. I could see her keel boarding tackle slung beneath her, ready to be lowered to the deck of a quarry when once her grappling hooks had seized the prey. Doubtless they were already manning the latter, and as soon as we were beneath her the steel tentacles would reach down and seize us as her crew swarmed down the boarding tackle to our deck.

I called Hovan Du and he crept back to my side where I whispered my instructions in his ear. When I was done he nodded his head with a low growl. I cast off the harness hook that held me to the deck, and the ape and I moved to our bow after I had issued brief, whispered instructions to Gor Hajus and Dar Tarus. We were now almost directly beneath the enemy craft; I could see the grappling hooks being prepared for lowering. Our bow ran beneath the stern of the other ship and the moment was at hand for which I had been waiting. Now those upon the deck of the patrol boat could not see Hovan Du or me. The boarding tackle of the other ship swung fifteen feet above our heads; I whispered a word of command to the ape and simultaneously we crouched and sprang for the tackle. It may sound like a mad chance—failure meant almost certain death—but I felt that if two of us could reach the deck of the patrol boat while her crew was busy with the grappling gear it would be well worth the risk.

Gor Hajus had assured me that there would not be more than six men aboard the patrol ship; that one would be at the controls and the others manning the grappling hooks. It would be a most propitious time to gain a footing on the enemy's deck.

Hovan Du and I made our leaps and Fortune smiled upon us, though the huge ape but barely reached the tackle with one outstretched hand, while my Earthly muscles carried me easily to my goal. Together we made our way rapidly towards the bow of the patrol craft and without hesitation, and as previously arranged, he clambered quickly up the starboard side and I the port. If I were the more agile jumper Hovan Du far outclassed me in climbing, with the result that he reached the rail and was clambering over while my eyes were still below the level of the deck, which was, perhaps a fortunate thing for me since, by chance, I had elected to gain the deck directly at a point where, unknown to me, one of the crew of the ship was engaged with the grappling hooks. Had his eyes not been attracted elsewhere by the shout of one of his fellows who was first to see Hovan Du's savage face rise above the gunwale, he could have dispatched me with a single blow before ever I could have set foot upon the deck.

The ape had also come up directly in front of a Toonolian warrior and this fellow had let out a yell of surprise and sought to draw his sword, but the ape, for all his great bulk, was too quick for him; and as my eyes topped the rail I saw the mighty anthropoid seize the unfortunate man by the harness, drag him to the side and hurl him to destruction far below. Instantly we were both over the rail and squarely on deck while the remaining members of the craft's crew, abandoning their stations, ran forward to overpower us. I think that the sight of the great, savage beast must have had a demoralizing effect upon them, for they hesitated, each seeming to be willing to accord his fellow the honour of first engaging us; but they did come on, though slowly. This hesitation I was delighted to see, for it accorded perfectly with the plan that I had worked out, which depended largely upon the success which might attend the efforts of Gor Hajus and Dar Tarus to reach the deck of the patrol when our craft had risen sufficiently close beneath the other to permit them to reach the boarding tackle, which we were utilizing with reverse English, as one might say.

Gor Hajus had cautioned me to dispatch the man at the controls as quickly as possible, since his very first act would be to injure them the instant that there appeared any possibility that we might be successful in our attempt to take his ship, and so I ran quickly towards him and before he could draw I cut him down. There were now four against us and we waited for them to advance that we might gain time for our fellows to reach the deck.

The four moved slowly forward and were almost within

striking distance when I saw Gor Hajus' head appear above the stern rail, quickly followed by that of Dar Tarus.

'Look!' I cried to the enemy, 'and surrender,' and I pointed astern.

One of them turned to look and what he saw brought an exclamation of surprise to his lips. 'It is Gor Hajus,' he cried, and then, to me: 'What is your purpose with us if we surrender?'

'We have no quarrel with you,' I replied. 'We but wish to leave Toonol and go our way in peace—we shall not harm you.'

He turned to his fellows while, at a sign from me, my three companions stopped their advance and waited. For a few minutes the four warriors conversed in low tones, then he who had first spoken addressed me.

'There are few Toonolians,' he said, 'who would not be glad to serve Gor Hajus, whom we had thought long dead, but to surrender our ship to you would mean certain death for us when we reported our defeat at our headquarters. On the other hand were we to continue our defence most of us here upon the deck of this flier would be killed. If you can assure us that your plans are not aimed at the safety of Toonol I can make a suggestion that will afford an avenue of escape and safety for us all.'

'We only wish to leave Toonol,' I replied. 'No harm can come to Toonol because of what I seek to accomplish.'

'Good! and where do you wish to go?'

'That I may not tell you.'

'You may trust us, if you accept my proposal,' he assured me, 'which is that we convey you to your destination, after which we can return to Toonol and report that we engaged you and that after a long running fight, in which two of our number were killed, you eluded us in the darkness and escaped.'

'Can we trust these men?' I asked, addressing Gor Hajus, who assured me that we could, and thus the compact was entered into which saw us speeding rapidly towards Phundahl aboard one of Vobis Kan's own fliers.

PHUNDAHL

THE following night the Toonolian crew set us down just inside the wall of the city of Phundahl, following the directions of Dar Tarus who was a native of the city, had been a warrior of the Jeddara's Guard and, prior to that, seen service in Phundahl's tiny navy. That he was familiar with every detail of Phundahl's defences and her systems of patrols was evidenced by the fact that we landed without detection, and that the Toonolian ship rose and departed apparently unnoticed.

Our landing place had been the roof of a low building built within and against the city wall. From this roof Dar Tarus led us down an inclined runway to the street, which, at this point, was quite deserted. The street was narrow and dark, being flanked upon one side by the low buildings built against the city wall and upon the other by higher buildings, some of which were windowless and none showing any light. Dar Tarus explained that he had chosen this point for our entrance because it was a district of storage houses, and while a hive of industry during the day, was always deserted at night, not even a watchman being required owing to the almost total absence of thievery upon Barsoom.

By devious and roundabout ways he led us finally to a section of second rate shops, eating places and hotels such as are frequented by the common soldiers, artisans and slaves, where the only attention we attracted was due to the curiosity aroused by Hovan Du. As we had not eaten since leaving Mu Tel's palace, our first consideration was food. Mu Tel had furnished Gor Hajus with money, so that we had the means to gratify our wants. Our first stop was at a small shop where Gor Hajus purchased four or five pounds of thoat steak for Hovan Du, and then we repaired to an eating place of which Dar Tarus knew. At first the proprietor would not let us bring Hovan Du inside, but finally, after much argument, he permitted us to lock the great ape in an inner room where Hovan Du was forced to remain with his thoat meat while we sat at a table in the outer room.

I will say for Hovan Du that he played his role well, nor was there once when the proprietor of the place, or any of his patrons, or the considerable crowd that gathered to listen to the altercation, could have guessed that the body of the great, savage beast was animated by a human brain. It was really only when feeding or fighting that the simian half of Hovan Du's brain appeared to exercise any considerable influence upon him yet there seemed little doubt that it always coloured all his thoughts and actions to some extent, accounting for his habitual taciturnity and the quickness with which he was aroused to anger, as well as to the fact that he never smiled, nor appeared to appreciate in any degree the humour of a situation. He assured me, however, that the human half of his brain not only appreciated but greatly enjoyed the lighter episodes and occurrences of our adventure and the witty stories and anecdotes related by Gor Hajus, the assassin, but that his simian anatomy had developed no muscles wherewith to evidence physical expression of his mental reactions.

We dined heartily, though upon rough and simple fare, but were glad to escape the prying curiosity of the garrulous and gossipy proprietor, who plied us with so many questions as to our past performances and future plans that Dar Tarus, who was our spokesman here, was hard put to it to quickly fabricate replies that would be always consistent. However, escape we did at last, and once again in the street, Dar Tarus set out to lead us to a public lodging house of which he knew. As we went we approached a great building of wondrous beauty in and out of which constant streams of people were pouring, and when we were before it Dar Tarus asked us to wait without as he must enter. When I asked him why, he told me that this was a temple of Tur, the god worshipped by the people of Phundahl.

'I have been away for a long time,' he said, 'and have had no opportunity to do honour to my god. I shall not keep you waiting long. Gor Hajus, will you loan me a few pieces of gold?'

In silence the Toonolian took a few pieces of money from one of his pocket pouches and handed them to Dar Tarus, but I could see that it was only with difficulty that he hid an expression of contempt, since the Toonolians are atheists.

I asked Dar Tarus if I might accompany him into the temple, which seemed to please him very much; and so we fell in with the stream approaching the broad entrance. Dar Tarus gave me two of the gold pieces that he had borrowed from Gor Hajus and told me to follow directly behind him and do whatever I saw him doing. Directly inside the main entrance, and spread entirely across it at intervals that permitted space for the worshippers to pass between them, was a line of priests, their entire bodies including their heads and faces, covered by a mantle of white cloth. In front of each was a substantial stand upon which rested a cash drawer. As we approached one of these we handed him a piece of gold which he immediately changed into many pieces of lesser value, one of which we dropped into a box at his side whereupon he made several passes with his hands above our heads, dipped one of his fingers into a bowl of dirty water which he rubbed upon the ends of our noses, mumbled a few words which I could not understand and turned to the next in line as we passed on into the interior of the great temple. Never have I seen such a gorgeous display of wealth and lavish ornamentation as confronted my eyes in this, the first of the temples of Tur that it was my fortune to behold.

The enormous floor was unbroken by a single pillar and arranged upon it at regular intervals were carven images resting upon gorgeous pedestals. Some of these images were of men and some of women and many of them were beautiful; and there were others of beasts and of strange, grotesque creatures and many of these were hideous indeed. The first we approached was that of a beautiful female figure; and about the pedestal of this lay a number of men and women prone upon the floor against which they bumped their heads seven times and then arose and dropped a piece of money into a receptacle provided for that purpose, moving on then to another figure. The next that Dar Tarus and I visited was that of a man with the body of a *silian*, about the pedestal of which was arranged a series of horizontal wooden bars in concentric circles. The bars were about five feet from the floor and hanging from them by their knees were a number of men and women repeating monotonously, over and over again, something that sounded to me like, *bibble-babble-blup*.

Dar Tarus and I swung to the bars like the others and mumbled the meaningless phrase for a minute or two, then we swung down, dropped a coin into the box, and moved on. I asked Dar Tarus what the words were that we had repeated and what they meant, but he said he did not know. I asked him if anyone knew, but he appeared shocked and said that such a question was sacrilegious and revealed a marked lack of faith. At the next figure we visited the people were all upon their hands and knees crawling madly in a circle about the pedestal. Seven times around they crawled and then they arose and put some money in a dish and went their ways. At another the people rolled about, saying, 'Tur is Tur; Tur is Tur; Tur is Tur,' and dropping money in a golden bowl when they were done.

'What god was that?' I whispered to Dar Tarus when we had quit this last figure, which had no head, but eyes, nose and mouth in the centre of its belly.

'There is but one god,' replied Dar Tarus, solemnly, 'and he is Tur!'

'Was that Tur?' I inquired.

'Silence, man,' whispered Dar Tarus. 'They would tear you to pieces were they to hear such heresy.'

'Oh, I beg your pardon,' I exclaimed. 'I did not mean to offend. I see now that that is merely one of your idols.'

Dar Tarus clapped a hand over my mouth. 'S-s-s-t!' he cautioned to silence. 'We do not worship idols—there is but one god and he is Tur!'

'Well, what are these?' I insisted, with a sweep of a hand that embraced the several score images about which were gathered the thousands of worshippers.

'We must not ask,' he assured me. 'It is enough that we have faith that all the works of Tur are just and righteous. Come! I shall soon be through and we may join our companions.'

He led me next to the figure of a monstrosity with a mouth that ran entirely around its head. It had a long tail and the breasts of a woman. About this image were a great many people, each standing upon his head. They also were repeating over and over, 'Tur is Tur; Tur is Tur; Tur is Tur.' When we had done this for a minute or two, during which I had a devil of a time maintaining my equilibrium, we arose, dropped a coin into the box by the pedestal and moved on.

'We may go now,' said Dar Tarus. 'I have done well in the sight of Tur.'

'I notice,' I remarked, 'that the people repeated the same phrase before this figure that they did at the last—Tur is Tur.'

'Oh, no,' exclaimed Dar Tarus. 'On the contrary they said just exactly the opposite from what they said at the other. At that they said, Tur is Tur; while at this they turned it right around backwards, which makes a very great difference.'

'It sounded the same to me,' I insisted.

'That is because you lack faith,' he said sadly, and we passed out of the temple after depositing the rest of our money in a huge chest, of which there were many standing about almost filled with coins.

We found Gor Hajus and Hovan Du awaiting us impatiently, the centre of a large and curious throng among which were many warriors in the metal of Xaxa, the Jeddara of Phundahl. They wanted to see Hovan Du perform, but Dar Tarus told them that he was tired and in an ugly mood.

'Tomorrow,' he said, 'when he is rested I shall bring him out upon the avenues to amuse you.'

With difficulty we extricated ourselves, and passing into a quieter avenue, took a roundabout way to the lodging place, where Hovan Du was confined in a small chamber while Gor Hajus, Dar Tarus and I were conducted by slaves to a large sleeping apartment where sleeping silks and furs were arranged for us upon a low platform that encircled the room and was broken only at the single entrance to the chamber. Here were already sleeping a considerable number of men, while two armed slaves patrolled the aisle to guard the guests from assassins.

It was still early and some of the other lodgers were conversing in low whispers so I sought to engage Dar Tarus in conversation relative to his religion, about which I was curious.

'The mysteries of religions always fascinate me, Dar Tarus,' I told him.

'Ah, but that is the beauty of the religion of Tur,' he exclaimed, 'it has no mysteries. It is simple, natural, scientific and every word and work of it is susceptible of proof through the pages of Turgan, the great book written by Tur himself.

'Tur's home is upon the sun. There, one hundred thousand years go, he made Barsoom and tossed it out into space. Then he amused himself by creating man in various forms and two sexes; and later he fashioned animals to be food for man and each other, and caused vegetation and water to appear that man and the animals might live. Do you not see how simple and scientific it all is?'

But it was Gor Hajus who told me most about the religion of Tur one day when Dar Tarus was not about. He said that the Phundahlians maintained that Tur still created every living thing with his own hands. They denied vigorously that man possessed the power to reproduce his kind and taught their young that all such belief was vile; and always they hid every evidence of natural procreation, insisting to the death that even those things which they witnessed with their own eyes and experienced with their own bodies in the bringing forth of their young never transpired.

Turgan taught them that Barsoom is flat and they shut their minds to every proof to the contrary. They would not leave Phundahl far for fear of falling off the edge of the world; they would not permit the development of aeronautics because should one of their ships circumnavigate Barsoom it would be a wicked sacrilege in the eyes of Tur who made Barsoom flat.

They would not permit the use of telescopes, for Tur taught them that there was no other world than Barsoom and to look at another would be heresy; nor would they permit the teaching in their schools of any history of Barsoom that antedated the creation of Barsoom by Tur, though Barsoom has a well authenticated written history that reaches back more than one hundred thousand years; nor would they permit any geography of Barsoom except that which appears in Turgan, nor any scientific researches along biological lines. Turgan is their only text book—if it is not in Turgan it is a wicked lie.

Much of all this and a great deal more I gathered from one source or another during my brief stay in Phundahl, whose people are, I believe, the least advanced in civilization of any of the red nations upon Barsoom. Giving, as they do, all their best thought to religious matters, they have become ignorant, bigoted and narrow, going as far to one extreme as the Toonolians do to the other.

However, I had not come to Phundahl to investigate her culture but to steal her queen, and that thought was uppermost in my mind when I awoke to a new day—my first in Phundahl. Following the morning meal we set out in the direction of the palace to reconnoitre, Dar Tarus leading us to a point from which he might easily direct us the balance of the way, as he did not dare accompany us to the immediate vicinity of the royal grounds for fear of recognition, the body he now possessed having formerly belonged to a well-known noble.

It was arranged that Gor Hajus should act as spokesman and I as keeper of the ape. This arranged, we bade farewell to Dar Tarus and set forth, the three of us, along a broad and beautiful avenue that led directly to the palace gates. We had been planning and rehearsing the parts that we were to play and which we hoped would prove so successful that they would open the gates to us and win us to the presence of the Jeddara.

As we strolled with seeming unconcern along the avenue, I had ample opportunity to enjoy the novel and beautiful sights of this rich boulevard of palaces. The sun shone down upon vivid scarlet lawns, gorgeous flowered pimalia and a score of other rarely beautiful Barsoomian shrubs and trees, while the avenue itself was shaded by almost perfect specimens of the magnificent sorapus. The sleeping apartments of the buildings had all been lowered to their daytime level, and from a hundred balconies gorgeous silks and furs were airing in the sun. Slaves were briskly engaged with their duties about the grounds, while upon many a balcony women and children sat at their morning meal. Among the children we aroused considerable enthusiasm, or at least Hovan Du did, nor was he without interest to the adults. Some of them would have detained us for an exhibition, but we moved steadily on towards the palace, for nowhere else had we business or concern within the walls of Phundahl.

Around the palace gates was the usual crowd of loitering curiosity seekers; for after all human nature is much the same everywhere, whether skins be black or white, red or yellow or brown, upon Earth or upon Mars. The crowd before Xaxa's gates was largely made up of visitors from the islands of that part of the Great Toonolian Marshes which owes allegiance to Phundahl's queen, and like all provincials eager for a glimpse of royalty; though none the less to be interested by the antics of a simian, wherefore we had a ready made audience awaiting our arrival. Their natural fear of the great brute caused them to fall back a little at our approach so that we had a clear avenue to the very gates themselves, and there we halted while the crowds closed in behind, forming a half circle about us. Gor Hajus addressed them in a loud tone of voice that might be overheard by the warriors and their officers beyond the gates, for it was really them we had come to entertain, not the crowds in which we had not the slightest interest.

'Men and women of Phundahl,' cried Gor Hajus, 'behold two poor panthans, who, risking their lives, have captured and trained one of the most savage and ferocious and at the same time most intelligent specimens of the great white ape of Barsoom ever before seen in captivity and at great expense have brought it to Phundahl for your entertainment and edification. My friends, this wonderful ape is endowed with human intelligence; he understands every word that is spoken to him. With your kind attention, my friends, I will endeavour to demonstrate the remarkable intelligence of this ferocious, man-eating beast—an intelligence that has entertained the crowned heads of Barsoom and mystified the minds of her most learned savants.'

I thought Gor Hajus did pretty well as a bally-hoo artist. I had to smile as I listened, here upon Mars, to the familiar lines that I had taught him out of my Earthly experience of county fairs and amusement parks, so highly ludicrous they sounded falling from the lips of the Assassin of Toonol; but they evidently interested his auditors and impressed them, too, for they craned their necks and stood in earnest-eyed silence awaiting the performance of Hovan Du. Even better, several members of the Jeddara's Guard pricked up their ears and sauntered towards the gates; and among them was an officer.

Gor Hajus caused Hovan Du to lie down at word of

command, to get up, to stand upon one foot, and to indicate the number of fingers that Gor Hajus held up by growling once for each finger, thus satisfying the audience that he could count; but these simple things were only by way of leading up to the more remarkable achievements which we hoped would win an audience before the Jeddara. Gor Hajus borrowed a set of harness and weapons from a man in the crowd and had Hovan Du don it and fence with him, and then indeed did we hear exclamations of amazement.

The warriors and the officer of Xaxa had drawn near the gates and were interested spectators, which was precisely what we wished, and now Gor Hajus was ready for the final, astounding revelation of Hovan Du's intelligence.

'These things that you have witnessed are as nothing,' he cried. 'Why, this wonderful beast can even read and write. He was captured in a deserted city near Ptarth and can read and write the language of that country. Is there among you one who, by chance, comes from that distant country?'

A slave spoke up. 'I am from Ptarth.'

'Good!' said Gor Hajus. 'Write some simple instructions and hand them to the ape. I will turn my back that you may know that I cannot assist him in any way.'

The slave drew forth a tablet from a pocket pouch and wrote briefly. What he wrote he handed to Hovan Du. The ape read the message and without hesitation moved quickly to the gate and handed it to the officer standing upon the other side, the gate being constructed of wrought metal in fanciful designs that offered no obstruction to the view or to the passage of small articles. The officer took the message and examined it.

'What does it say?' he demanded of the slave that had penned it.

'It says,' replied the latter: 'Take this message to the officer who stands just within the gates.'

There were exclamations of surprise from all parts of the crowd and Hovan Du was compelled to repeat his performance several times with different messages which directed him to do various things, the officer always taking a great interest in the proceedings.

'It is marvellous,' said he at last. 'The Jeddara would be amused by the performance of this beast. Wait here, therefore, until I have sent word to her that she may, if she so desires, command your presence.'

Nothing could have better suited us and so we waited with what patience we might for the messenger to return; and while we waited Hovan Du continued to mystify his audience with new proofs of his great intelligence.

XAXA

The officer returned, the gates swung out and we were commanded to enter the courtyard of the palace of Xaxa, Jeddara of Phundahl. After that events transpired with great rapidity—surprising and totally unexpected events. We were led through an intricate maze of corridors and chambers until I became suspicious that we were purposely being confused, and convinced that whether such was the intention or not the fact remained that I could no more have retraced my steps to the outer courtyard than I could have flown without wings. We had planned that, in the event of gaining admission to the palace, we would carefully note whatever might be essential to a speedy escape; but when, in a whisper, I asked Gor Hajus if he could find his way out again he assured me that he was as confused as I.

The palace was in no sense remarkable nor particularly interesting, the work of the Phundahlian artists being heavy and oppressing and without indication of high imaginative genius. The scenes depicted were mostly of a religious nature illustrating passages from Turgan, the Phundahlian bible, and, for the most part, were a series of monotonous repetitions. There was one, which appeared again and again, depicting Turgan creating a round, flat Mars and hurling it into Space, that always reminded me of a culinary artist turning a flapjack in a Child's window.

There were also numerous paintings of what appeared to be court scenes delineating members of the Phundahlian royal line in various activities; it was noticeable that the more recent ones in which Xaxa appeared had had the principal figure repainted so that there confronted me from time to time portraits, none too well done, of the beautiful face and figure of Valla Dia in the royal trappings of a jeddara. The effect of these upon me is not easy of description. They brought home to me the fact that I was approaching and should presently be face to face with, the person of the woman to whom I had consecrated my love and my life, and yet in that same person I should be confronting one whom I loathed and would destroy.

We were halted at last before a great door and from the number of warriors and nobles congregated before it I was confident that we were soon to be ushered into the presence of the Jeddara. As we waited those assembled about us eyed us with, it seemed to me, more of hostility than curiosity and when the door swung open they accompanied us, with the exception of a few warriors, into the chamber beyond. The room was of medium size and at the farther side, behind a massive table, sat Xaxa. About her were grouped a number of heavily armed nobles. As I looked them over I wondered if among them was he for whom the body of Dar Tarus had been filched; for we had promised him that if conditions were favourable we would attempt to recover it.

Xaxa eyed us coldly as we were halted before her. 'Let us see the beast perform,' she commanded, and then suddenly: 'What mean you by permitting strangers to enter my presence bearing arms?' she cried. 'Sag Or, see that their weapons are removed!' and she turned to a handsome young warrior standing near her.

Sag Or! That was the name. Before me stood the noble for whom Dar Tarus had suffered the loss of his liberty, his body and his love. Gor Hajus had also recognized the name and Hovan Du, too; I could tell by the way they eyed the man as he advanced. Curtly he instructed us to hand our weapons to two warriors who advanced to receive them. Gor Hajus hesitated. I admit that I did not know what course to pursue.

Everyone seemed hostile and yet that might be, and doubtless was, but a reflection of their attitude towards all strangers. If we refused to disarm we were but three against a roomful, if they chose to resort to force; or if they turned us out of the palace because of it we would be robbed of this seemingly god-given opportunity to win to the very heart of Xaxa's palace and to her very presence, where we must eventually win before we could strike. Would such an opportunity ever be freely offered us again? I doubted it and felt that we had better assume a vague risk now than, by refusing their demand, definitely arm their suspicions. So I quietly removed my weapons and handed them to the warrior waiting to receive them; and following my example, Gor Hajus did likewise, though I can imagine with what poor grace.

Once again Xaxa signified that she would see Hovan Du perform. As Gor Hajus put him through his antics she watched listlessly; nor did anything that the ape did arouse the slightest flicker of interest among the entire group assembled about the Jeddara. As the thing dragged on I became obsessed with apprehensions that all was not right. It seemed to me that an effort was being made to detain us for some purpose—to gain time. I could not understand, for instance, why Xaxa required that we repeat several times the least interesting of the ape's performances. And all the time Xaxa sat playing with a long, slim dagger, and I saw that she watched me quite as much as she watched Hovan Du, while I found it difficult to keep my eyes averted from that perfect face, even though I knew that it was but a stolen mask behind which lurked the cruel mind of a tyrant and a murderess.

At last came an interruption to the performance. The door opened and a noble entered who went directly to the Jeddara, whom he addressed briefly and in a low tone. I saw that she asked him several questions and that she seemed vexed by his replies. Then she dismissed him with a curt gesture and turned towards us.

'Enough of this!' she cried. Her eyes rested upon mine and she pointed her slim dagger at me. 'Where is the other?' she demanded.

'What other?' I inquired.

'There were three of you, beside the ape. I know nothing about the ape, nor where, nor how you acquired it; but I do know all about you, Vad Voro, and Gor Hajus, the Assassin of Toonol, and Dar Tarus. Where is Dar Tarus?' her voice was low and musical and entirely beautiful—the voice of Valla Dia—but behind it I knew was the terrible personality of Xaxa, and I knew too that it would be hard to deceive her, for she must have received what information she had directly from Ras Thavas. It had been stupid of me not to foresee that Ras Thavas would immediately guess the purpose of my mission and warn Xaxa. I perceived instantly that it would be worse than useless to deny our identity, rather I must explain our presence—if I could.

'Where is Dar Tarus?' she repeated.

'How should I know?' I countered. 'Dar Tarus has reasons to believe that he would not be safe in Phundahl and I imagine that he is not anxious that anyone should know his whereabouts—myself included. He helped me to escape from the Island of Thavas, for which his liberty was to be his reward. He has not chosen to accompany me further upon my adventures.'

Xaxa seemed momentarily disarmed that I did not deny my identity—evidently she had supposed that I would do so.

'You admit then,' she said, 'that you are Vad Varo, the assistant of Ras Thavas?'

'Have I ever sought to deny it?'

'You have disguised yourself as a red-man of Barsoom.'

'How could I travel in Barsoom otherwise, where every man's hand is against a stranger?'

'And why would you travel in Barsoom?' Her eyes narrowed as she waited for my reply.

'As Ras Thavas has doubtless sent you word, I am from another world and I would see more of this one,' I told her. 'Is that strange?'

'And you come to Phundahl and seek to gain entrance to my presence and bring with you the notorious Assassin of Toonol that you may see more of Barsoom?'

'Gor Hajus may not return to Toonol,' I explained, 'and so he must seek service for his sword at some other court than that of Vobis Kan—in Phundahl perhaps, or if not here he must move on. I hope that he will decide to accompany me as I am a stranger in Barsoom, unaccustomed to the manners and ways of her people. I would fare ill without a guide and mentor.'

'You shall fare ill,' she cried. 'You have seen all of Barsoom that you are destined to see—you have reached the end of your adventure. You think to deceive me, eh? You do not know, perhaps, that I have heard of your infatuation for Valla Dia or that I am fully conversant with the purpose of your visit to Phundahl.' Her eyes left me and swept her nobles and her warriors. 'To the pits with them!' she cried. 'Later we shall choose the manner of their passing.'

Instantly we were surrounded by a score of naked blades. There was no escape for Gor Hajus or me, but I thought that I saw an opportunity for Hovan Du to get away. I had had the possibility of such a contingency in mind from the first and always I had been on the lookout for an avenue of escape for one of us, and so the open windows at the right of the Jedda had not gone unnoticed, nor the great trees growing in the courtyard beneath. Hovan Du was close beside me as Xaxa spoke.

'Go!' I whispered. 'The windows are open. Go, and tell Dar Tarus what has happened to us,' and then I fell back away from him and dragged Gor Hajus with me as though we would attempt to resist arrest and while I thus distracted their attention from him Hovan Du turned towards an open window. He had taken but a few steps when a warrior attempted to halt him; with that the ferocious brain of the anthropoid seemed to seize dominion over the great creature. With a hideous growl he leaped with the agility of a cat upon the unfortunate Phundahlian, swung him high in giant hands and using his body as a flail tumbled his fellows to right and left as he cut a swath towards the open window nearest him.

Instantly pandemonium reigned in the apartment. The attention of all seemed centred upon the great ape and even those who had been confronting us turned to attack Hovan Du. And in the midst of the confusion I saw Xaxa step to some heavy hangings directly behind her desk, part them and disappear.

'Come!' I whispered to Gor Hajus. Apparently intent only upon watching the conflict between the ape and the warriors I moved forward with the fighters but always to the left towards the desk that Xaxa had just quitted. Hovan Du was giving a good account of himself. He had discarded his first victim and one by one had seized others as they came within range of his long arms and powerful hands, sometimes four at a time as he stood well braced upon two of his hand-like feet and fought with the other four. His shock of bristling hair stood erect upon his skull and his fierce eyes blazed with rage as, towering high above his antagonists, he fought for his life—the most feared of all the savage creatures of Barsoom. Perhaps his greatest advantage lay in the inherent fear of him that was a part of every man in that room who faced him, and it forwarded my quickly conceived plan, too, for it kept every eye turned upon Hovan Du, so that Gor Hajus and I were able to work our way to the rear of the desk. I think Hovan Du must have sensed my intention then, for he did the one thing best suited to attract every eye from us to him and, too, he gave me notice that the human half of his brain was still alert and watchful of our welfare.

Heretofore the Phundahlians must have looked upon him as a remarkable specimen of great ape, marvellously trained, but now, of a sudden, he paralysed them with awe, for his roars and growls took the form of words and he spoke with the tongue of a human. He was near the window now. Several of the nobles were pushing bravely forward. Among them was Sag Or. Hovan Du reached forth and seized him, wrenching his weapons from him. 'I go,' he cried: 'but let harm befall my friends and I shall return and tear the heart from Xaxa. Tell her that, from the Great Ape of Ptarth.'

For an instant the warriors and the nobles stood transfixed with awe. Every eye was upon Hovan Du as he stood there with the struggling figure of Sag Or in his mighty grasp. Gor Hajus and I were forgotten. And then Hovan Du turned and leaped to the sill of the window and from there lightly to the branches of the nearest tree; and with him went Sag Or, the favourite of Xaxa, the Jeddara. At the same instant I drew Gor Hajus with me between the hangings in the rear of Xaxa's desk, and as they fell behind us we found ourselves in the narrow mouth of a dark corridor.

Without knowledge of where the passage led we could only follow it blindly, urged on by the necessity for discovering a hiding place or an avenue of escape from the palace before the pursuit, which we knew would be immediately instituted, overtook us. As our eyes became accustomed to the gloom, which was partially dispelled by a faint luminosity, we moved more rapidly and presently came to a narrow spiral runway which descended into a dark hole below the level of the corridor and also arose into equal darkness above.

'Which way?' I asked Gor Hajus.

'They will expect us to descend,' he replied, 'for in that direction lies the nearest avenue of escape.'

'Then we will go up.'

'Good!' he exclaimed. 'All we seek now is a place to hide until night has fallen, for we may not escape by day.'

We had scarcely started to ascend before we heard the first sound of pursuit—the clank of accoutrements in the corridor beneath. Yet, even with this urge from behind, we were forced to move with great caution, for we knew not what lay before. At the next level there was a doorway, the door closed and locked, but there was no corridor, nor anywhere to hide, and so we continued on upwards. The second level was identical with that just beneath, but at the third a single corridor ran straight off into darkness and at our right was a door, ajar. The sounds of pursuit were appreciably nearer now and the necessity for concealment seemed increasing as the square of their growing proportions until every other consideration was overwhelmed by it. Nor is this so strange when the purpose of my adventure is considered and that discovery now must assuredly spell defeat and blast for ever the slender ray of hope that remained for the resurrection of Valla Dia in her own flesh.

There was scarce a moment for consideration. The corridor before us was shrouded in darkness—it might be naught but a blind alley. The door was close and ajar. I pushed it gently inward. An odour of heavy incense greeted our nostrils and through the small aperture we saw a portion of a large chamber garishly decorated. Directly before us, and almost wholly obstructing our view of the entire chamber, stood a colossal statue of a squatting man-like figure. Behind us we heard voices—our pursuers already were ascending the spiral—they would be upon us in a few seconds. I examined the door and discovered that it fastened with a spring lock. I looked again into the chamber and saw no one within the range of our vision, and then I motioned Gor Hajus to follow me and stepping into the room closed the door behind us. We had burned our bridges. As the door closed the lock engaged with a sharp, metallic click.

'What was that?' demanded a voice, originating seemingly, at the far end of the chamber.

Gor Hajus looked at me and shrugged his shoulders in resignation (he must have been thinking what I was thinking—that with two avenues we had chosen the wrong one) but he smiled and there was no reproach in his eyes.

'It sounded from the direction of the Great Tur,' replied a second voice.

'Perhaps someone is at the door,' suggested the first speaker.

Gor Hajus and I were flattened against the back of the statue that we might postpone as long as possible our inevitable discovery should the speakers decide to investigate the origin of the noise that had attracted their suspicions. I was facing against the polished stone of the figure's back, my hands outspread upon it. Beneath my fingers were the carven bits of its ornamental harness—jutting protuberances that were costly gems set in these trappings of stone, and there were gorgeous inlays of gold filagree; but these things I had no eyes for now. We could hear the two conversing as they came nearer. Perhaps I was nervous. I do not know. I am sure I never shrank from an encounter when either duty or expediency called; but in this instance both demanded that we avoid conflict and remain undiscovered. However that may be, my fingers must have been moving nervously over the jewelled harness of the figure when I became vaguely, perhaps subconsciously, aware that one of the gems was loose in its setting I do not recall that this made any impression upon my conscious mind, but I do know that it seemed to catch the attention of my wandering fingers and they must have paused to play with the loosened stone.

The voices seemed quite close now—it could be but a matter of seconds before we should be confronted by their owners. My muscles seemed to tense for the anticipated encounter and unconsciously I pressed heavily upon the loosened setting—whereat a portion of the figure's back gave noiselessly inward revealing to us the dimly lighted interior of the statue. We needed no further invitation; simultaneously we stepped across the threshold and in almost the same movement I turned and closed the panel gently behind us. I think that there was absolutely no sound connected with the entire transaction; and following it we remained in utter silence, motionless—scarce breathing. Our eyes became quickly accustomed to the dim interior which we discovered was lighted through numerous small orifices in the shell of the statue, which was entirely hollow, and through these same orifices every outside sound came clearly to our ears. We had scarcely closed the opening when we heard the voices directly outside it and simultaneously there came a hammering on the door by which we had entered the apartment from the corridor. 'Who seeks entrance to Xaxa's Temple?' demanded one of the voices within the room.

''Tis I, dwar of the Jeddara's Guard,' boomed a voice from without. 'We are seeking two who came to assassinate Xaxa.'

'Came they this way?'

'Think you, priest that I should be seeking them here had they not?'

'How long since?'

'Scarce twenty tals since,' replied the dwar.

'Then they are not here,' the priest assured him, 'for we have been here for a full zode* and no other has entered the temple during that time. Look quickly to Xaxa's apartments above and to the roof and the hangars, for if you followed them up the spiral there is no other where they might flee.'

'Watch then the temple carefully until I return,' shouted the warrior and we heard him and his men moving on up the spiral.

Now we heard the priests conversing as they moved slowly past the statue. 'What could have caused the noise that first attracted our attention?' asked one.

'Perhaps the fugitives tried the door,' suggested the other.

'It must have been that, but they did not enter or we should have seen them when they emerged from behind the Great Tur, for we were facing him at the time, nor have once turned our eyes from this end of the temple.'

'Then at least they are not within the temple.'

'And where else they may be is no concern of ours.'

'No, nor if they reached Xaxa's apartment, if they did not pass through the temple.'

'Perhaps they did reach it.'

'And they were assassins!'

'Worse things might befall Phundahl.'

'Hush! the gods have ears.'

'Of stone.'

* A tal is about one second, and a zode approximately two and one-half hours, Earth time.

'But the ears of Xaxa are not of stone and they hear many things that are not intended for them.'

'The old she-banth!'

'She is Jeddara and High Priestess.'

'Yes, but——' the voices passed beyond the range of our ears at the far end of the temple, yet they had told me much—that Xaxa was feared and hated by the priesthood and that the priests themselves had none too much reverence for their deity, as evidenced by the remark of one that the gods have ears of stone. And they had told us other things, important things, when they conversed with the dwar of the Jeddara's Guard.

Gor Hajus and I now felt that we had fallen by chance upon a most ideal place of concealment, for the very guardians of the temple would swear that we were not, could not be, where we were. Already had they thrown the pursuers off our track.

Now, for the first time, we had an opportunity to examine our hiding place. The interior of the statue was hollow and far above us, perhaps forty feet, we could see the outside light shining through the mouth, ears and nostrils, just below which a circular platform could be discerned running around the inside of the neck. A ladder with flat rungs led upwards from the base to the platform. Thick dust covered the floor on which we stood, and the extremity of our position suggested a careful examination of this dust, with the result that I was at once impressed by the evidence that it revealed; which indicated that we were the first to enter the statue for a long time, possibly for years, as the fine coating of almost impalpable dust that covered the floor was undisturbed. As I searched for this evidence my eyes fell upon something lying huddled close to the base of the ladder and approaching nearer I saw that it was a human skeleton, while a closer examination revealed that the skull was crushed and one arm and several ribs broken. About it lay, dust-covered, the most gorgeous trappings I had ever seen. Its position at the foot of the ladder, as well as the crushed skull and broken bones, appeared quite conclusive evidence of the manner in which death had come—the man had fallen head foremost from the circular platform forty feet above, carrying with him to eternity, doubtless, the secret of the entrance to the interior of the Great Tur.

I suggested this to Gor Hajus who was examining the dead man's trappings and he agreed with me that such must have been the manner of his death.

'He was a high priest of Tur,' whispered Gor Hajus, 'and probably a member of the royal house—possibly a jeddak. He has been dead a long time.'

'I am going up above,' I said. 'I will test the ladder. If it is safe, follow me up. I think we shall be able to see the interior of the temple through the mouth of Tur.'

'Go carefully,' Gor Hajus admonished. 'The ladder is very old.'

I went carefully, testing each rung before I trusted my weight to it, but I found the old sorapus wood of which it was constructed sound and as stanch as steel. How the high priest came to his death must always remain a mystery, for the ladder or the circular platform would have carried the weight of a hundred red-men.

From the platform I could see through the mouth of Tur. Below me was a large chamber along the sides of which were ranged other, though lesser, idols. They were even more grotesque than those I had seen in the temple in the city and their trappings were rich beyond the conception of man—Earthman—for the gems of Barsoom scintillate with rays unknown to us and of such gorgeous and blinding beauty as to transcend description. Directly in front of the Great Tur was an altar of palthon, a rare and beautiful stone, blood red, in which are traced in purest white Nature's most fanciful designs; the whole vastly enhanced by the wondrous polish which the stone takes beneath the hand of the craftsman.

Gor Hajus joined me and together we examined the interior of the temple. Tall windows lined two sides, letting in a flood of light. At the far end, opposite the Great Tur, were two enormous doors, closing the main entrance to the chamber, and here stood the two priests whom we had heard conversing. Otherwise the temple was deserted. Incense burned upon tiny altars before each of the minor idols, but whether any burned before the Great Tur we could not see.

Having satisfied our curiosity relative to the temple, we returned our attention to a further examination of the interior of Tur's huge head and were rewarded by the discovery of another ladder leading upwards against the rear wall to a higher and smaller platform that evidently led to the eyes. It did not take me long to investigate and here I found a most comfortable chair set before a control that operated the eyes, so that they could be made to turn from side to side, or up or down, according to the whim of the operator; and here too was a speaking-tube leading to the mouth. This again I must needs investigate and so I returned to the lower platform and there I discovered a device beneath the tongue of the idol, and this device, which was in the nature of an amplifier, was connected with the speaking-tube from above. I could not repress a smile as I considered these silent witnesses to the perfidy of man and thought of the broken thing lying at the foot of the ladder. Tur, I could have sworn, had been silent for many years.

Together Gor Hajus and I returned to the higher platform and again I made a discovery—the eyes of Tur were veritable periscopes. By turning them we could see any portion of the temple and what we saw through the eyes was magnified. Nothing could escape the eyes of Tur and presently, when the priests began to talk again, we discovered that nothing could escape Tur's ears, for every slightest sound in the temple came clearly to us. What a valuable adjunct to high priesthood this Great Tur must have been in the days when that broken skeleton lying below us was a thing of blood and life!

THE GREAT TUR

THE day dragged wearily for Gor Hajus and me. We watched the various priests who came in pairs at intervals to relieve those who had preceded them, and we listened to their prattle, mostly idle gossip of court scandals. At times they spoke of us and we learned that Hovan Du had escaped with Sag Or, nor had they been located as yet, nor had Dar Tarus. The whole court was mystified by our seemingly miraculous disappearance. Three thousand people, the inmates and attachés of the palace, were constantly upon the lookout for us. Every part of the palace and the palace grounds had been searched and searched again. The pits had been explored more thoroughly than they had been explored within the memory of the oldest retainer, and it seemed that queer things had been unearthed there—things of which not even Xaxa dreamed; and the priests whispered that at least one great and powerful house would fall because of what a dwar of the Jeddara's Guard had discovered in a remote precinct of the pits.

As the sun dropped below the horizon and darkness came, the interior of the temple was illuminated by a soft white light, brilliantly, but without the glare of Earthly artificial illumination. More priests came and many young girls, priestesses. They performed before the idols, chanting meaningless gibberish. Gradually the chamber filled with worshippers, nobles of the Jeddara's court with their women and their retainers, forming in two lines along either side of the temple before the lesser idols, leaving a wide aisle from the great entrance to the foot of the Great Tur and towards this aisle they all faced, waiting. For what were they waiting? Their eyes were turned expectantly towards the closed doors of the great entrance and

Gor Hajus and I felt our eyes held there too, fascinated by the suggestion that they were about to open and reveal some stupendous spectacle.

And presently the doors did swing slowly open and all we saw was what appeared to be a great roll of carpet lying upon its side across the opening. Twenty slaves, naked but for their scant leather harness, stood behind the huge roll; and as the doors swung fully open they rolled the carpet inward to the very feet of the altar before the Great Tur, covering the wide aisle from the entranceway almost to the idol with a thick, soft rug of gold and white and blue. It was the most beautiful thing in the temple, where all else was blatant, loud and garish, or hideous, or grotesque. And then the doors closed and again we waited; but not for long. Bugles sounded from without, the sound increasing as they neared the entrance. Once more the doors swung in. Across the entrance stood a double rank of gorgeously trapped nobles. Slowly they entered the temple and behind them came a splendid chariot drawn by two banths, the fierce Barsoomian lion, held in leash by slaves on either side. Upon the chariot was a litter and in the litter, reclining at ease, lay Xaxa. As she entered the temple the people commenced to chant her praises in a monotonous sing-song. Chained to the chariot and following on foot was a red warrior and behind him a procession composed of fifty young men and an equal number of young girls.

Gor Hajus touched my arm. 'The prisoner,' he whispered, 'do you recognize him?'

'Dar Tarus!' I exclaimed.

It was Dar Tarus—they had discovered his hiding place and arrested him, but what of Hovan Du? Had they taken him, also? If they had it must have been only after slaying him, for they never would have sought to capture the fierce beast, nor would he have brooked capture. I looked for Sag Or, but he was nowhere to be seen within the temple and this fact gave me hope that Hovan Du might be still at liberty.

The chariot was halted before the altar and Xaxa alighted; the lock that held Dar Tarus's chain to the vehicle was opened and the banths were led away by their attendants to one side of the temple behind the lesser idols. Then Dar Tarus was dragged roughly to the altar and thrown upon it and Xaxa, mounting the steps at its base, came close to his side and with hands outstretched above him looked up at the Great Tur towering above her. How beautiful she was! How richly trapped! Ah, Valla Dia! that your sweet form should be debased to the cruel purposes of the wicked mind that now animates you!

Xaxa's eyes now rested upon the face of the Great Tur. 'O Tur, Father of Barsoom,' she cried, 'behold the offering we place before you, All-seeing, All-knowing, All-powerful One, and frown no more upon us in silence. For a hundred years you have not deigned to speak aloud to your faithful slaves; never since Hora San, the high priest, was taken away by you on that long gone night of mystery have you unsealed your lips to your people. Speak, Great Tur! Give us some sign, ere we plunge this dagger into the heart of our offering, that our works are pleasing in thine eyes. Tell us whither went the two who came here today to assassinate your high priestess; reveal to us the fate of Sag Or. Speak, Great Tur, ere I strike,' and she raised her slim blade above the heart of Dar Tarus and looked straight upwards into the eyes of Tur.

And then, as a bolt from the blue, I was struck by the great inspiration. My hand sought the lever controlling the eyes of Tur and I turned them until they completed a full circuit of the room and rested upon Xaxa. The effect was magical. Never before had I seen a whole room full of people so absolutely stunned and awestruck as were these. As the eyes returned to Xaxa she seemed turned to stone and her copper skin to have taken on an ashen purple hue. Her dagger remained stiffly poised above the heart of Dar Tarus. Not for a hundred years had they seen the eyes of the Great Tur move. Then I placed the speaking-tube to my lips and the voice of Tur rumbled through the chamber. As from one great throat a gasp arose from the crowded temple floor and the people fell upon their knees and buried their faces in their hands.

'Judgement is mine!' I cried. 'Strike not lest ye be struck! To Tur is the sacrifice!'

I was silent then, attempting to plan how best to utilize the advantage I had gained. Fearfully, one by one, the bowed heads were raised and frightened eyes sought the face of Tur. I gave them another thrill by letting the god's eyes wander slowly over the upturned faces, and while I was doing this I had another inspiration, which I imparted to Gor Hajus in a low whisper. I could hear him chuckle as he started down the ladder to carry my new plan into effect. Again I had recourse to the speaking-tube.

'The sacrifice is Tur's,' I rumbled. 'Tur will strike with his own hand. Extinguish the lights and let no one move under pain of instant death until Tur gives the word. Prostrate yourselves and bury your eyes in your palms, for whosoever sees shall be blinded when the spirit of Tur walks among his people.'

Down they went again and one of the priests hurriedly extinguished the lights, leaving the temple in total darkness and while Gor Hajus was engaged with his part of the performance I tried to cover any accidental noise he might make by keeping up a running fire of celestial revelation.

'Xaxa, the high priestess, asks what has become of the two whom she believed came to assassinate her. I, Tur, took them to myself. Vengeance is Tur's! And Sag Or I took; also. In the guise of a great ape I came and took Sag Or and none knew me; though even a fool might have guessed, for who is there ever heard a great ape speak with tongue of man unless he was animated by the spirit of Tur?'

I guess that convinced them, it being just the sort of logic suited to their religion, or it would have convinced them if they had not already been convinced. I wondered what might be passing in the mind of the doubting priest who had remarked that the gods had ears of stone.

Presently I heard a noise upon the ladder beneath me and a moment later someone climbed upon the circular landing.

'All's well,' whispered the voice of Gor Hajus. 'Dar Tarus is with me.'

'Light the temple!' I commanded through the speaking-tube. 'Rise and look upon your altar.'

The lights flashed on and the people rose, trembling, to their feet. Every eye was bent upon the altar and what they saw there seemed to crush them with terror. Some of the women screamed and fainted. It all impressed me with the belief that none of them had taken this god of theirs with any great amount of seriousness, and now when they were confronted with absolute proof of his miraculous powers they were swept completely off their feet. Where, a few moments before, they had seen a live sacrifice awaiting the knife of the high priestess they saw now only a dust-covered human skull. I grant you that without an explanation it might have seemed a miracle to almost anyone, so quickly had Gor Hajus run from the base of the idol with the skull of the dead high priest and returned again leading Dar Tarus with him. I had been a bit concerned as to what the attitude of Dar Tarus might be, who was no more conversant with the hoax than were the Phundahlians, but Gor Hajus had whispered, 'For Valla Dia' in his ear and he had understood and come quickly.

'The Great Tur,' I now announced, 'is angry with his people. For a long time they have denied him in their hearts even while they made open worship of him. The Great Tur is angry with Xaxa. Only through Xaxa may the people of Phundahl be saved from destruction, for the Great Tur is angry. Go then from the temple and the palace leaving no human being here other than Xaxa, the high priestess of Tur. Leave her here in solitude beside the altar. Tur would speak with her alone.'

I could see Xaxa fairly shrivel in fright.

'Is the Jeddara Xaxa, High Priestess of the Great God Tur, afraid to meet her master?' I demanded. The woman's jaw trembled so that she could not reply. 'Obey! or Xaxa and all her people shall be struck dead!' I fairly screamed at them.

Like cattle they turned and fled towards the entrance and Xaxa, her knees shaking so that she could scarce stand erect, staggered after them. A noble saw her and pushed her roughly back, but she shrieked and ran after him when he had left her. Then others dragged her to the foot of the altar and threw her roughly down and one menaced her with his sword, but at that I called aloud that no harm must befall the Jeddara if they did not wish the wrath of Tur to fall upon them all. They left her lying there and so weak from fright was she that she could not rise, and a moment later the temple was empty, but not until I had shouted after them to clear the whole palace within a quarter zode, for my plan required a free and unobstructed as well as unobserved field of action.

The last of them was scarce out of sight ere we three descended from the head of Tur and stepped out upon the temple floor behind the idol. Quickly I ran towards the altar, upon the other side of which Xaxa had dropped to the floor in a swoon. She still lay there and I gathered her into my arms and ran quickly back to the door in the wall behind the idol—the doorway through which Gor Hajus and I had entered the temple earlier in the day.

Preceded by Gor Hajus and followed by Dar Tarus, I ascended the runway towards the roof where the conversation of the priests had informed us were located the royal hangars. Had Hovan Du and Sag Or been with us my cup of happiness would have been full, for within half a day what had seemed utter failure and defeat had been turned almost to assured success. At the landing where lay Xaxa's apartments we halted and looked within, for the long night voyage I contemplated would be cold and the body of Valla Dia must be kept warm with suitable robes even though it was inhabited by the spirit of Xaxa. Seeing no one we entered and soon found what we required. As I was adjusting a heavy robe of orluk about the Jeddara she regained consciousness. Instantly she recognized me and then Gor Hajus and finally Dar Tarus. Mechanically she felt for her dagger, but it was not there, and when she saw my smile she paled with anger. At first she must have jumped to the conclusion that she had been the victim of a hoax, but presently a doubt seemed to enter her mind—she must have been recalling some of the things that had transpired within the temple of the Great Tur, and these, neither she nor any other mortal might explain.

'Who are you?' she demanded.

'I am Tur,' I replied, brazenly.

'What is your purpose with me?'

'I am going to take you away from Phundahl,' I replied.

'But I do not wish to go. You are not Tur. You are Vad Varo. I shall call for help and my guards will come and slay you.'

'There is no one in the palace,' I reminded her. 'Did I, Tur, not send them away?'

'I shall not go with you,' she announced firmly. 'Rather would I die.'

'You shall go with me, Xaxa,' I replied, and though she fought and struggled we carried her from her apartment and up the spiral runway to the roof where, I prayed, I should find the hangars and the royal fliers; and as we stepped out into the fresh night air of Mars we did see the hangars before us, but we saw something else—a group of Phundahlian warriors of the Jeddara's Guard whom they had evidently failed to notify of the commands of Tur. At sight of them Xaxa cried aloud in relief. 'To me! To the Jeddara!' she cried. 'Strike down these assassins and save me!'

There were three of them and there were three of us, but they were armed and between us we had but Xaxa's slender dagger. Gor Hajus carried that. Victory seemed turned to defeat as they rushed towards us, but it was Gor Hajus who gave them pause. He seized Xaxa and raised the blade, its point above her heart. 'Halt!' he cried, 'or I strike.'

The warriors hesitated; Xaxa was silent, stricken with fear. Thus we stood in stalemate when, just beyond the three Phundahlian warriors, I saw a movement at the roof's edge. What was it? In the dim light I saw something that seemed a human head, and yet unhuman, rise slowly above the edge of the roof, and then, silently, a great form followed, and then I recognized it—Hovan Du, the great white ape.

'Tell them,' I cried to Xaxa in a loud voice that Hovan Du might hear, 'that I am Tur, for see, I come again in the semblance of a white ape!' and I pointed to Hovan Du. 'I would not destroy these poor warriors. Let them lay down their weapons and go in peace.'

The men turned, and seeing the great ape standing there behind them, materialized, it might have been, out of thin air, were shaken.

'Who is he, Jeddara?' demanded one of the men.

'It is Tur,' replied Xaxa in a weak voice; 'but save me from him! Save me from him!'

'Throw down your weapons and your harness and fly!' I commanded, 'or Tur will strike you dead. Heard you not the people rushing from the palace at Tur's command? How think you we brought Xaxa hither with a lesser power than Tur's when all her palace was filled with her fighting men? Go, while yet you may in safety.'

One of them unbuckled his harness and threw it with his weapons upon the roof, and as he started at a run for the spiral his companions followed his example. Then Hovan Du approached us.

'Well done, Vad Varo,' he growled, 'though I know not what it is all about.'

'That you shall know later,' I told him, 'but now we must

find a swift flier and be upon our way. Where is Sag Or? Does he still live?'

'I have him securely bound and safely hidden in one of the high towers of the palace,' replied the ape. 'It will be easy to get him when we have launched a flier.'

Xaxa was eyeing us ragefully. 'You are not Tur!' she cried. 'The ape has exposed you.'

'But too late to profit you in any way, Jeddara,' I assured her. 'Nor could you convince one of your people who stood in the temple this night that I am not Tur. Nor do you, yourself, know that I am not. The ways of Tur, the all-powerful, all-knowing, are beyond the conception of mortal man. To you then, Jeddara, I am Tur, and you will find me all-powerful enough for my purposes.'

I think she was still perplexed as we found and dragged forth a flier, aboard which we placed her, and turned the craft's nose towards a lofty tower where Hovan Du told us lay Sag Or. 'I shall be glad to see myself again,' said Dar Tarus, with a laugh.

'And you shall be yourself again, Dar Tarus,' I told him, 'as soon as ever we can come again to the pits of Ras Thavas.'

'Would that I might be reunited with my sweet Kara Vasa,' he sighed. 'Then, Vad Varo, the last full measure of my gratitude would be yours.'

'Where may we find her?'

'Alas, I do not know. It was while I was searching for her that I was apprehended by the agents of Xaxa. I had been to her father's palace only to learn that he had been assassinated and his property confiscated. The whereabouts of Kara Vasa they either did not know or would not divulge; but they held me there upon one pretext or another until a detachment of the Jeddara's Guard could come and arrest me.'

'We shall have to make inquiries of Sag Or,' I said.

We were now coming to a stop alongside a window of the tower Hovan Du had indicated, and he and Dar Tarus leaped to the sill and disappeared within. We were all armed now, having taken the weapons discarded by the three warriors at the hangars, and with a good flier beneath our feet and all our little company reunited, with Xaxa and Sag Or, whom they were now conducting aboard, we were indeed in high spirits.

As we got under way again, setting our nose towards the east, I asked Sag Or if he knew what had become of Kara Vasa, but he assured me, in surly tones, that he did not.

'Think again, Sag Or,' I admonished him, 'and think hard, for perhaps upon your answer your life depends.'

'What chance have I for life?' he sneered, casting an ugly look towards Dar Tarus.

'You have every chance,' I replied. 'Your life lies in the hollow of my hand; and you serve me well it shall be yours, though in your own body and not in that belonging to Dar Tarus.'

'You do not intend destroying me?'

'Neither you nor Xaxa,' I answered. 'Xaxa shall live on in her own body and you in yours.'

'I do not wish to live in my own body,' snapped the Jeddara.

Dar Tarus stood looking at Sag Or—looking at his own body like some disembodied soul—as weird a situation as I have ever encountered.

'Tell me, Sag Or,' he said, 'what has become of Kara Vasa. When my body has been restored to me and yours to you I shall hold no enmity against you if you have not harmed Kara Vasa and will tell me where she be.'

'I cannot tell you, for I do not know. She was not harmed, but the day after you were assassinated she disappeared from Phundahl. We were positive that she was spirited away by her father, but from him we could learn nothing. Then he was assassinated,' the man glanced at Xaxa, 'and since, we have learned nothing. A slave told us that Kara Vasa, with some of her father's warriors, had embarked upon a flier and set out for Helium, where she purposed placing herself under the protection of the great War Lord of Barsoom; but of the truth of that we know nothing. This is the truth. I, Sag Or, have spoken!'

It was futile then to search Phundahl for Kara Vasa and so we held our course towards the east and the Tower of Thavas.

BACK TO THAVAS

ALL that night we sped beneath the hurtling moons of Mars, as strange a company as was ever foregathered upon any planet, I will swear. Two men, each possessing the body of the other, an old and wicked empress whose fair body belonged to a youthful damsel beloved by another of this company, a great white ape dominated by half the brain of a human being, and I, a creature of a distant planet, with Gor Hajus, the Assassin of Toonol, completed the mad roster.

I could scarce keep my eyes from the fair form and face of Xaxa, and it is well that I was thus fascinated for I caught her in the act of attempting to hurl herself overboard, so repugnant to her was the prospect of living again in her own old and hideous corpse. After that I kept her securely bound and fastened to the deck, though it hurt me to see the bonds upon those fair limbs.

Dar Tarus was almost equally fascinated by the contemplation of his own body, which he had not seen for many years.

'By my first ancestor,' he ejaculated. 'It must be that I was the least vain of fellows, for I give you my word I had no idea I was so fair to look upon. I can say this now without seeming egotism, since I am speaking of Sag Or,' and he laughed aloud at his little joke.

But the fact remained that the body and face of Dar Tarus were beautiful indeed, though there was a hint of steel in the eyes and the set of the jaw that betokened fighting blood. Little wonder, then, that Sag Or had coveted the body of this young warrior; for his own, which Dar

Tarus now possessed, was marked by dissipation and age; nor that Dar Tarus yearned to come again into his own.

Just before dawn we dropped to one of the numerous small islands that dot the Great Toonolian Marshes and nosing the ship between the boles of great trees we came to rest upon the surface of the ground, half buried in the lush and gorgeous jungle grasses, well hidden from the sight of possible pursuers. Here Hovan Du found fruits and nuts for us which the simian section of his brain pronounced safe for human consumption, and instinct led him to a nearby spring from which there bubbled delicious water. We four were half famished and much fatigued, so that the food and water were most welcome to us; nor did Xaxa and Sag Or refuse them. Having eaten, three of us lay down upon the ship's deck to sleep, after securely chaining our prisoners, while the fourth stood watch. In this way, taking turns, we slept away most of the day and when night fell, rested and refreshed, we were ready to resume our flight.

Making a wide detour to the south we avoided Toonol and about two hours before dawn we sighted the high Tower of Thavas. I think we were all keyed up to the highest pitch of excitement, for there was not one aboard that flier but whose whole life would be seriously affected by the success or failure of our venture. As a first precaution we secured the hands of Xaxa and Sag Or behind their backs and placed gags in their mouths, lest they succeed in giving warning of our approach.

Cluros had long since set and Thuria was streaming towards the horizon as we stopped our motor and drifted without lights a mile or two south of the tower while we waited impatiently for Thuria to leave the heavens to darkness and the world to us. To the north-west the lights of Toonol shone plainly against the dark background of the sky, and there were lights too in some of the windows of the great laboratory of Ras Thavas, but the tower itself was dark from plinth to pinnacle.

And now the nearer moon dropped plummet-like beneath the horizon and left the scene to darkness and to us. Dar Tarus started the motor, the wonderful, silent motor of Barsoom, and we moved slowly, close to the ground, towards Ras Thavas' island, with no sound other than the gentle whirring of our propeller; nor could that have been heard scarce a hundred feet so slowly was it turning. Close off the island we came to a stop behind a cluster of giant trees and Hovan Du, going into the bow, uttered a few low growls. Then we stood waiting in silence, listening. There was a rustling in the dense undergrowth upon the shore. Again Hovan Du voiced his low, grim call and this time there came an answer from the black shadows. Hovan Du spoke in the language of the great apes and the invisible creature replied.

For five minutes, during which time we were aware from the different voices that others had joined in the conversation from the shore, the apes conversed, and then Hovan Du turned to me.

'It is arranged,' he said. 'They will permit us to hide our ship beneath these trees and they will permit us to pass out again when we are ready and board her, nor will they harm us in any way. All they ask is that when we are through we shall leave the gate open that leads to the inner court.'

'Do they understand that while an ape goes in with us none will return with us?' I asked.

'Yes, but they will not harm us.'

'Why do they wish the gate left open?'

'Do not inquire too closely, Vad Varo,' replied Hovan Du. 'It should be enough that the great apes make it possible for you to restore Valla Dia's body to her brain and escape with her from this terrible place.'

'It is enough,' I replied. 'When may we land?'

'At once. They will help us drag the ship beneath the trees and make her fast.'

'But first we must top the wall to the inner court,' I reminded him.

'Yes, true—I had forgotten that we cannot open the gate from this side.'

He spoke again, then, to the apes, whom we had not yet seen; and then he told me that all was arranged and that he and Dar Tarus would return with the ship after landing us inside the wall.

Again we got under way and rising slowly above the outer wall dropped silently to the courtyard beyond. The night was unusually dark, clouds having followed Thuria and blotted out the stars after the moon had set. No one could have seen the ship at a distance of fifty feet, and we moved almost without noise. Quietly we lowered our prisoners over the side and Gor Hajus and I remained with them while Dar Tarus and Hovan Du rose again and piloted the ship back to its hiding place.

I moved at once to the gate and, unlatching it, waited. I heard nothing. Never, I think, have I endured such utter silence. There came no sound from the great pile rising behind me, nor any from the dark jungle beyond the wall. Dimly I could see the huddled forms of Gor Hajus, Xaxa and Sag Or beside me—otherwise I might have been alone in the darkness and immensity of space.

It seemed an eternity that I waited there before I heard a soft scratching on the panels of the heavy gate. I pushed it open and Dar Tarus and Hoven Du stepped silently within as I closed and relatched it. No one spoke. All had been carefully planned so that there was no need of speech. Dar Tarus and I led the way, Gor Hajus and Hovan Du brought up the rear with the prisoners. We moved directly to the entrance to the tower, found the runway and descended to the pits. Every fortune seemed with us. We met no one, we had no difficulty in finding the vault we sought, and once within we secured the door so that we had no fear of interruption—that was our first concern—and then I hastened to the spot where I had hidden Valla Dia behind the body of a large warrior, tucked far back against the wall in a dark corner. My heart stood still as I dragged aside the body of the warrior, for always had I feared that Ras Thavas, knowing my interest in her and guessing the purpose of my venture, would cause every chamber and pit to be searched and every body to be examined until he found her for whom he sought; but my fears had been baseless, for there lay the body of Xaxa, the old and wrinkled casket of the lovely brain of my beloved, where I had hidden it against this very night. Gently I lifted it out and bore it to one of the two ersite topped tables. Xaxa, standing there bound and gagged, looked on with eyes that shot hate and loathing at me and at that hideous body to which her brain was so soon to be restored.

As I lifted her to the adjoining slab she tried to wriggle from my grasp and hurl herself to the floor, but I held her and soon had strapped her securely in place. A moment later she was unconscious and the re-transference was well under way. Gor Hajus, Sag Or and Hovan Du were interested spectators, but to Dar Tarus, who stood ready to assist me, it was an old story, for he had worked in the laboratory and seen more than enough of similar operations. I will not bore you with a description of it—it was but a repetition of what I had done many times in preparation for this very event.

At last it was completed and my heart fairly stood still as I replaced the embalming fluid with Valla Dia's own life blood and saw the colour mount to her cheeks and her rounded bosoms rise and fall to her gentle breathing. Then she opened her eyes and looked up into mine.

'What has happened, Vad Varo?' she asked. 'Has something gone amiss that you have recalled me so soon, or did I not respond to the fluid?'

Her eyes wandered past me to the faces of the others standing about. 'What does it mean?' she asked. 'Who are these?'

I raised her gently in my arms and pointed at the body of Xaxa lying deathlike on the ersite slab beside her. Valla Dia's eyes went wide. 'It is done?' she cried, and clapped her hands to her face and felt of all her features and of the soft, delicate contours of her smooth neck; and yet she could scarce believe it and asked for a glass and I took one from Xaxa's pocket pouch and handed it to her. She looked long into it and the tears commenced to roll down her cheeks, and then she looked up at me through the mist of them and put her dear arms about my neck and drew my face down to hers. 'My chieftain,' she whispered—that was all. But it was enough. For those two words I had risked my life and faced unknown dangers, and gladly would I risk my life again for that same reward and always, for ever.

Another night had fallen before I had completed the restoration of Dar Tarus and Hovan Du. Xaxa and Sag Or and the great ape I left sleeping the death-like sleep of Ras Thavas' marvellous anaesthetic. The great ape I had no intention of restoring, but the others I felt bound to return to Phundahl, though Dar Tarus, now resplendent in his own flesh and the gorgeous trappings of Sag Or, urged me not to inflict them again upon the long suffering Phundahlians.

'But I have given my word,' I told him.

'Then they must be returned,' he said.

'Though what I may do afterwards is another matter,' I

added, for there had suddenly occurred to me a bold scheme.

I did not tell Dar Tarus what it was nor would I have had time, for at that very instant we heard someone without trying the door and then we heard voices and presently the door was tried again, this time with force. We made no noise, but just waited. I hoped that whoever it was would go away. The door was very strong and when they tried to force it they must soon have realized the futility of it because they quickly desisted and we heard their voices for only a short time thereafter and then they seemed to have gone away.

'We must leave,' I said, 'before they return.'

Strapping the hands of Xaxa and Sag Or behind them and placing gags in their mouths I quickly restored them to life, nor ever did I see two less grateful. The looks they cast upon me might well have killed could looks do that, and with what disgust they viewed one another was writ plain in their eyes.

Cautiously unbolting the door I opened it very quietly, a naked sword in my right hand and Dar Tarus, Gor Hajus and Hovan Du ready with theirs at my shoulder, and as it swung back it revealed two standing in the corridor watching—two of Ras Thavas' slaves and one of them was Yamdor, his body servant. At sight of us the fellow gave a loud cry of recognition and before I could leap through the doorway and prevent they had both turned and were flying up the corridor as fast as their feet would carry them.

Now there was no time to be lost—everything must be sacrificed to speed. Without thought of caution or silence we hastened through the pits towards the runway in the tower; and when we stepped into the inner court it was night again, but the farther moon was in the heavens and there were no clouds. The result was that we were instantly discovered by a sentry who gave the alarm as he ran forward to intercept us.

What was a sentry doing in the courtyard of Ras Thavas? I could not understand. And what were these? A dozen armed warriors were hurrying across the court on the heels of the sentry.

'Toonolians!' shouted Gor Hajus. 'The warriors of Vobis Kan, Jeddak of Toonol!'

Breathlessly we raced for the gate. If we could but reach it first! But we were handicapped by our prisoners, who held back the moment they discovered how they might embarrass us, and so it was that we all met in front of the gate. Dar Tarus and Gor Hajus and Hovan Du and I put Valla Dia and our prisoners behind us and fought the twenty warriors of Toonol with the odds five to one against us; but we had more heart in the fight than they and perhaps that gave us an advantage, though I am sure that Gor Hajus was as ten men himself so terrible was the effect of his name alone upon the men of Toonol.

'Gor Hajus!' cried one, the first to recognize him.

'Yes, it is Gor Hajus,' replied the assassin. 'Prepare to meet your ancestors!' and he drove into them like a racing propeller, and I was upon his right and Hovan Du and Dar Tarus upon his left.

It was a pretty fight, but it must eventually have gone against us, so greatly were we outnumbered, had I not thought of the apes and the gate beside us. Working my way to it I threw it open and there upon the outside, attracted by the noise of the conflict, stood a full dozen of the great beasts. I called to Gor Hajus and the others to fall back beside the gate, and as the apes rushed in I pointed to the Toonolian warriors.

I think the apes were at a loss to know which were friends and which were foes, but the Toonolians apprised them by attacking them, while we stood aside with our points upon the ground. Just a moment we stood thus waiting. Then as the apes rushed among the Toonolian warriors, we slipped into the darkness of the jungle beyond the outer wall and sought our flier. Behind us we could hear the growls and the roars of the beasts mingled with the shouts and the curses of the men; and the sound still rose from the courtyard as we clambered aboard the flier and pushed off into the night.

As soon as we felt that we were safely escaped from the Island of Thavas I removed the gags from the mouths o Xaxa and Sag Or and I can tell you that I immediately regretted it, for never in my life had I been subjected to such horrid abuse as poured from the wrinkled old lips of the Jeddara and it was only when I started to gag her again that she promised to desist.

My plans were now well laid and they included a return

to Phundahl since I could not start for Duhor with Valla Dia without provisions and fuel; nor could I obtain these elsewhere than in Phundahl since I felt that I held the key that would unlock the resources of that city to me; whereas all Toonol was in arms against us owing to Vobis Kan's fear of Gor Hajus.

So we retraced our way towards Phundahl as secretly as we had come, for I had no mind to be apprehended before we had gained entrance to the palace of Xaxa.

Again we rested over daylight upon the same island that had given us sanctuary two days before, and at dark we set out upon the last leg of our journey to Phundahl. If there had been pursuit we had seen naught of it; and that might easily be explained by the great extent of the uninhabited marshes across which we flew and the far southerly course that we followed close above the ground.

As we neared Phundahl I caused Xaxa and Sag Or to be again gagged, and further, I had their heads bandaged so that none might recognize them; and then we sailed straight over the city towards the palace, hoping that we would not be discovered and yet ready in the event that we should be.

But we came to the hangars on the roof apparently unseen and constantly I coached each upon the part he was to play. As we were settling slowly to the roof Dar Tarus, Hovan Du and Vall Dia quickly bound Gor Hajus and me and wrapped our heads in bandages, for we had seen below the figures of the hangar guard. Had we found the roof unguarded the binding of Gor Hajus and me had been unnecessary.

As we dropped nearer one of the guard hailed us. 'What ship?' he cried.

'The royal flier of the Jeddar of Phundahl,' replied Dar Tarus, 'returning with Xaxa and Sag Or.'

The warriors whispered among themselves as we dropped nearer and I must confess that I felt a bit nervous as to the outcome of our ruse; but they permitted us to land without a word and when they saw Villa Dia they saluted her after the manner of Barsoom, as, with the regal carriage of an empress, she descended from the deck of the flier.

'Carry the prisoners to my apartments!' she commanded, addressing the guard, and with the help of Hovan Du and

Dar Tarus the four bound and muffled figures were carried from the flier down the spiral runway to the apartments of Xaxa, Jeddara of Phundahl. Here excited slaves hastened to do the bidding of the Jeddara. Word must have flown through the palace with the speed of light that Xaxa had returned, for almost immediately court functionaries began to arrive and be announced; but Valla Dia sent word that she would see no one for a while. Then she dismissed her slaves, and at my suggestion Dar Tarus investigated the apartments with a view to finding a safe hiding place for Gor Hajus, me, and the prisoners. This he soon found in a small ante-chamber directly off the main apartment of the royal suite; the bonds were removed from the assassin and myself and together we carried Xaxa and Sag Or into the room.

The entrance here was furnished with a heavy door over which there were hangings that completely hid it. I bade Hovan Du, who, like the rest of us, wore Phundahlian harness, stand guard before the hangings and let no one enter but members of our own party. Gor Hajus and I took up our positions just within the hangings through which we cut small holes that permitted us to see all that went on within the main chamber, for I was greatly concerned for Valla Dia's safety while she posed as Xaxa, whom I knew to be both feared and hated by her people and therefore always liable to assassination.

Valla Dia summoned the slaves and bade them admit the officials of the court, and as the doors opened fully a score of nobles entered. They appeared ill at ease and I could guess that they were recalling the episode in the temple when they had deserted their jeddara and even hurled her roughly at the feet of the Great Tur, but Valla Dia soon put them at their ease.

'I have summoned you,' she said, 'to hear the word of Tur. Tur would speak again to his people. Three days and three nights have I spent with Tur. His anger against Phundahl is great. He bids me summon all the higher nobles to the temple after the evening meal tonight, and all the priests, and the commanders and dwars of the Guard, and as many of the lesser nobles as be in the palace; and then shall the people of Phundahl hear the word and the law of Tur and all those who shall obey shall live and all those who shall not obey shall die and woe be to him who, having been summoned, shall not be in the temple this night. I, Xaxa, Jeddara of Phundahl, have spoken! Go!'

They went and they seemed glad to go. Then Valla Dia summoned the odwar of the Guard, who would be in our world a general, and she told him to clear the palace of every living being from the temple level to roof an hour before the evening meal, nor to permit anyone to enter the temple or the levels above it until the hour appointed for the assembling in the temple to hear the word of Tur, excepting however those who might be in her own apartments, which were not to be entered upon pain of death. She made it all very clear and plain and the odwar understood and I think he trembled a trifle, for all were in great fear of the Jeddara Xaxa; and then he went away and the slaves were dismissed and we were alone.

JOHN CARTER

HALF an hour before the evening meal we carried Xaxa and Sag Or down the spiral runway and placed them in the base of the Great Tur and Gor Hajus and I took our places on the upper platform behind the eyes and voice of the idol. Valla Dia, Dar Tarus and Hovan Du remained in the royal apartment. Our plans were well formulated. There was no one between the door at the rear of the Great Tur and the flier that lay ready on the roof in the event that we were forced to flee through any miscarriage of our mad scheme.

The minutes dragged slowly by and darkness fell. The time was approaching. We heard the doors of the temple open and beyond we saw the great corridor brilliantly lighted. It was empty except for two priests who stood hesitating nervously in the doorway. Finally one of them mustered up sufficient courage to enter and switch on the lights. More bravely now they advanced and prostrated themselves before the altar of the Great Tur. When they arose and looked up into the face of the idol I could not resist the temptation to turn those huge eyes until they had rolled completely about the interior of the chamber and rested again upon the priests; but I did not speak and I think the effect of the awful silence in the presence of the living god was more impressive than would words have been. The two priests simply collapsed. They slid to the floor and lay there trembling, moaning and supplicating Tur to have mercy on them, nor did they rise before the first of the worshippers arrived.

Thereafter the temple filled rapidly and I could see that the word of Tur had been well and thoroughly disseminated. They came as they had before but there were more this time, and they ranged upon either side of the central aisle and there they waited, their eyes divided between the doorway and the god. About the time that I thought the next scene was about to be enacted I let Tur's eyes travel over the assemblage that they might be keyed to the proper pitch for what was to follow. They reacted precisely as had the priests, falling upon the floor and moaning and supplicating; and there they remained until the sounds of bugles announced the coming of the Jeddara. Then they rose unsteadily to their feet. The great doors swung open and there was the carpet and the slaves behind it. As they rolled it down towards the altar the bugles sounded louder and the head of the royal procession came into view. I had ordered it thus to permit of greater pageantry than was possible when the doors opened immediately upon the head of the procession. My plan permitted the audience to see the royal retinue advancing down the long corridor and the effect was splendid. First came the double rank of nobles and behind these the chariot drawn by two banths, bearing the litter upon which reclined Valla Dia. Behind her walked Dar Tarus, but all within that room thought they were looking upon the Jeddara Xaxa and her favourite, Sag Or. Hovan Du walked behind Sag Or and following came the fifty young men and the fifty maidens.

The chariot halted before the altar and Valla Dia descended and knelt and the voices that had been chanting the praises of Xaxa were stilled as the beautiful creature extended her hands towards the Great Tur and looked up into his face.

'We are ready, Master!' she cried. 'Speak! We await the word of Tur!'

A gasp arose from the kneeling assemblage, a gasp that ended in a sob. I felt that they were pretty well worked up and that everything ought to go off without a hitch. I placed the speaking-tube to my lips.

'I am Tur!' I thundered and the people trembled. 'I come to pass judgement on the men of Phundahl. As you receive my word so shall you prosper or so shall you perish. The sins of the people may be atoned by two who have sinned most in my sight.' I let the eyes of Tur rove about over the audience and then brought them to rest upon Valla Dia. 'Xaxa, are you ready to atone for your sins and the sins of your people?'

Valla Dia bowed her beautiful head. 'Thy will is law, Master!' she replied.

'And, Sag Or,' I continued, 'you have sinned. Are you prepared to pay?'

'As Tur shall require,' said Dar Tarus.

'Then it is my will,' I boomed, 'that Xaxa and Sag Or shall give back to those from whom they stole them, the beautiful bodies they now wear; that he from whom Sag Or took this body shall become Jeddak of Phundahl and High Priest of Tur; and that she from whom Xaxa stole her body shall be returned in pomp to her native country. I have spoken. Let any who would revolt against my word speak now or for ever hold his peace.'

There was no objection voiced. I had felt pretty certain that there would not be. I doubt if any god ever looked down upon a more subdued and chastened flock. As I had talked, Gor Hajus had descended to the base of the idol and removed the bonds from the feet and legs of Xaxa and Sag Or.

'Extinguish the light!' I commanded. A trembling priest did my bidding.

Valla Dia and Dar Tarus were standing side by side before the altar when the lights went out. In the next minute they and Gor Hajus must have worked fast, for when I heard a low whistle from the interior of the idol's base, the pre-arranged signal that Gor Hajus had finished his work, and ordered the lights on again, there stood Xaxa and Sag Or where Valla Dia and Dar Tarus had been, and the latter were nowhere in sight. I think the dramatic effect of that transformation upon the people there was the most stupendous thing I have ever seen. There was no cord or gag upon either Xaxa or Sag Or, nothing to indicate that they had been brought hither by force—no one about who might have so brought them. The illusion was perfect—it was a gesture of omnipotence that simply staggered the intellect. But I wasn't through.

'You have heard Xaxa renounce her throne,' I said, 'and Sag Or submit to the judgement of Tur.'

'I have not renounced my throne!' cried Xaxa. 'It is all a——'

'Silence!' I thundered. 'Prepare to greet the new jeddak, Dar Tarus of Phundahl!' I turned my eyes towards the great doors and the eyes of the assemblage followed mine.

They swung open and there stood Dar Tarus, resplendent in the trappings of Hora San, the long dead jeddak and high priest, whose bones we had robbed in the base of the idol an hour earlier. How Dar Tarus had managed to make the change so quickly is beyond me, but he had done it and the effect was colossal. He looked every inch a jeddak as he moved with slow dignity up the wide aisle along the blue and gold and white carpet. Xaxa turned purple with rage. 'Impostor!' she shrieked. 'Seize him! Kill him!' and she ran forward to meet him as though she would slay him with her bare hands.

'Take her away,' said Dar Tarus in a quiet voice, and at that Xaxa fell foaming to the floor. She shrieked and gasped and then lay still—a wicked old woman dead of apoplexy. And when Sag Or saw her lying there he must have been the first to realize that she was dead and that there was now no one to protect him from the hatreds that are levelled always at the person of a ruler's favourite. He looked wildly about for an instant and then threw himself at the feet of Dar Tarus.

'You promised to protect me!' he cried.

'None shall harm you,' replied Dar Tarus. 'Go your way and live in peace.' Then he turned his eyes upwards towards the face of the Great Tur. 'What is thy will, Master?' he cried. 'Dar Tarus, thy servant, awaits thy commands!'

I permitted an impressive silence before I replied.

'Let the priests of Tur, the lesser nobles and a certain number of the Jeddak's Guard go forth into the city and spread the word of Tur among the people that they may know that Tur smiles again upon Phundahl and that they have a new jeddak who stands high in the favour of Tur. Let the higher nobles attend presently in the chambers that were Xaxa's and do honour to Valla Dia in whose perfect body their Jeddara once ruled them, and effect the necessary arrangements for her proper return to Duhor, her native city. There also will they find two who have served Tur well and these shall be accorded the hospitality and friendship of every Phundahlian—Gor Hajus of Toonol and Vad Varo of Jasoom. Go! and when the last has gone let the temple be darkened. I, Tur, have spoken!'

Valla Dia had gone directly to the apartments of the former jeddara and the moment that the lights were extinguished Gor Hajus and I joined her. She could not wait to hear the outcome of our ruse, and when I assured her that there had been no hitch the tears came to her eyes for very joy.

'You have accomplished the impossible, my chieftain,' she murmured, 'and already can I see the hills of Duhor and the towers of my native city. Ah, Vad Varo, I had not dreamed that life might again hold for me such happy prospects. I owe you life and more than life.'

We were interrupted by the coming of Dar Tarus, and with him were Hovan Du and a number of the higher nobles. The latter received us pleasantly, though I think they were mystified as to just how we were linked with the service of their god nor, I am sure, did one of them ever learn. They were frankly delighted to be rid of Xaxa; and while they could not understand Tur's purpose in elevating a former warrior of the Guard to the throne, yet they were content if it served to relieve them from the wrath of their god, now a very real and terrible god, since the miracles that had been performed in the temple. That Dar Tarus had been of a noble family relieved them of embarrassment, and I noted that they treated him with great respect. I was positive that they would continue to treat him so, for he was also high priest and for the first time in a hundred years he would bring to the Great Tur in the Royal Temple the voice of god, for Hovan Du had agreed to take service with Dar Tarus, and Gor Hajus as well, so that there would never be lacking a tongue wherewith Tur might speak. I foresaw great possibilities for the reign of Dar Tarus, Jeddak of Phundahl.

At the meeting held in the apartments of Xaxa it was decided that Valla Dia should rest two days in Phundahl while a small fleet was preparing to transport her to Duhor. Dar Tarus assigned Xaxa's apartments for her use and gave her slaves from different cities to attend upon her, all of whom were to be freed and returned with Valla Dia to her native land.

It was almost dawn before we sought our sleeping silks and furs and the sun was high before we awoke. Gor Hajus and I breakfasted with Valla Dia, outside of whose door we had spread our beds that we might not leave her unprotected for a moment that it was not necessary. We had scarce finished our meal when a messenger came from Dar Tarus summoning us to the audience chamber, where we found some of the higher officers of the court gathered about the throne upon which Dar Tarus sat, looking every inch an emperor. He greeted us kindly, rising and descending from his dais to receive Valla Dia and escort her to one of the benches he had had placed beside the throne for her and for me.

'There is one,' he said to me, 'who has come to Phundahl overnight and now begs audience of the jeddak—one whom I thought you might like to meet again,' and he signed to one of his attendants to admit the petitioner; and when the doors at the opposite end of the room opened I saw Ras Thavas standing there. He did not recognize me or Valla Dia or Gor Hajus until he was almost at the foot of the throne, and when he did he looked puzzled and glanced again quickly at Dar Tarus.

'Ras Thavas of the Tower of Thavas. Toonol,' announced an officer.

'What would Ras Thavas of the Jeddak of Phundahl?' asked Dar Tarus.

'I came seeking audience of Xaxa,' replied Ras Thavas, 'not knowing of her death or your accession until this very morning; but I see Sag Or upon Xaxa's throne and beside him one whom I thought was Xaxa, though they tell me Xaxa is dead, and another who was my assistant at Thavas and one who is the Assassin of Toonol, and I am confused, Jeddak, and do not know whether I be among friends or foes.'

'Speak as though Xaxa still sat upon the throne of Phundahl,' Dar Tarus told him, 'for though I am Dar Tarus, whom you wronged, and not Sag Or, yet need you have no fear in the court of Phundahl.'

'Then let me tell you that Vobis Kan, Jeddak of Toonol, learning that Gor Hajus had escaped me, swore that I had set him free to assassinate him, and he sent warriors who took my island and would have imprisoned me had I not been warned in time to escape; and I came hither to Xaxa to beg her to send warriors to drive the men of Toonol from my island and restore it to me that I may carry on my scientific labours.'

Dar Tarus turned to me. 'Vad Varo, of all others you are most familiar with the work of Ras Thavas. Would you see him again restored to his island and his laboratory?'

'Only on condition that he devote his great skill to the

amelioration of human suffering,' I replied, 'and no longer prostitute it to the foul purposes of greed and sin.' This led to a discussion which lasted for hours, the results of which were of far-reaching significance. Ras Thavas agreed to all that I required and Dar Tarus commissioned Gor Hajus to head an army against Toonol.

But these matters, while of vast interest to those most directly concerned, have no direct bearing upon the story of my adventures upon Barsoom, as I had no part in them, since upon the second day I boarded a flier with Valla Dia and, escorted by a Phundahlian fleet, set out towards Duhor. Dar Tarus accompanied us for a short distance. When the fleet was stopped at the shore of the great marsh he bade us farewell and was about to step to the deck of his own ship and return to Phundahl when a shout arose from the deck of one of the other ships and word was soon passed that a lookout had sighted what appeared to be a great fleet far to the south-west. Nor was it long before it became plainly visible to us all and equally plain that it was headed for Phundahl.

Dar Tarus told me then that as much as he regretted it, there seemed nothing to do but return at once to his capital with the entire fleet, since he could not spare a single ship or man if this proved an enemy fleet, nor could Valla Dia or I interpose any objection; and so we turned about and sped as rapidly as the slow ships of Phundahl permitted, back towards the city.

The stranger fleet had sighted us at about the same time that we had sighted it, and we saw it change its course and bear down upon us; and as it came nearer it fell into single file and prepared to encircle us. I was standing at Dar Tarus' side when the colours of the approaching fleet became distinguishable and we first learned that it was from Helium.

'Signal and ask if they come in peace,' directed Dar Tarus.

'We seek word with Xaxa, Jeddara of Phundahl,' came the reply. 'The question of peace or war will be hers to decide.'

'Tell them that Xaxa is dead and that I, Dar Tarus, Jeddak of Phundahl, will receive the commander of Helium's fleet in peace upon the deck of this ship, or that I will receive him in war with all my guns. I, Dar Tarus, have spoken!'

From the bow of a great ship of Helium there broke the flag of truce and when Dar Tarus' ship answered it in kind the other drew near and presently we could see the men of Helium upon her decks. Slowly the great flier came alongside our smaller ship and when the two had been made fast a party of officers boarded us. They were fine-looking men, and at their head was one whom I recognized immediately though I never before had laid eyes upon him. I think he was the most impressive figure I have ever seen as he advanced slowly across the deck towards us—John Carter, Prince of Helium, War Lord of Barsoom.

'Dar Tarus,' he said, 'John Carter greets you and in peace, though it had been different, I think, had Xaxa still reigned.'

'You came to war upon Xaxa?' asked Dar Tarus.

'We came to right a wrong,' replied the Warlord. 'But from what we know of Xaxa that could have been done only by force.'

'What wrong has Phundahl done Helium?' demanded Dar Tarus.

'The wrong was against one of your own people—even against you in person.'

'I do not understand,' said Dar Tarus.

'There is one aboard my ship who may be able to explain to you, Dar Tarus,' replied John Carter, with a smile. He turned and spoke to one of his aides in a whisper, and the man saluted and returned to the deck of his own ship. 'You shall see with your own eyes, Dar Tarus.' Suddenly his eyes narrowed. 'This is indeed Dar Tarus who was a warrior of the Jeddara's Guard and supposedly assassinated by her command?'

'It is,' replied Dar Tarus.

'I must be certain,' said the War Lord.

'There is no question about it, John Carter,' I spoke up in English.

His eyes went wide, and when they fell upon me and he noted my lighter skin, from which the dye was wearing away, he stepped forward and held out his hand.

'A countryman?' he asked.

'Yes, an American,' I replied.

'I was almost surprised,' he said. 'Yet why should I be?

I have crossed—there is no reason why others should not. And you have accomplished it! You must come to Helium with me and tell me all about it.'

Further conversation was interrupted by the return of the aide, who brought a young woman with him. At sight of her Dar Tarus uttered a cry of joy and sprang forward, and I did not need to be told that this was Kara Vasa.

There is little more to tell that might not bore you in the telling—of how John Carter himself took Valla Dia and me to Duhor after attending the nuptials of Dar Tarus and Kara Vasa; and of the great surprise that awaited me in Duhor, where I learned for the first time that Kor San, Jeddak of Duhor, was the father of Valla Dia; and of the honours and the great riches that he heaped upon me when Valla Dia and I were wed.

John Carter was present at the wedding and we initiated upon Barsoom a good old American custom, for the War Lord acted as best man; and then he insisted that we follow that up with a honeymoon and bore us off to Helium, where I am writing this.

Even now it seems like a dream that I can look out of my window and see the scarlet and the yellow towers of the twin cities of Helium; that I have met, and see daily, Cathoris, Thuvia of Ptarth, Tara of Helium, Gahan of Gathol and that peerless creature, Dejah Thoris, Princess of Mars. Though to me, beautiful as she is, there is another even more beautiful—Valla Dia, Princess of Duhor—Mrs. Ulysses Paxton.